Rule No.2: No Questions

Happy Reading!

Mel

# Other Books in the Series

Rule No.1: Avoid Trouble

# Rule No.2:

## No Questions

Mel Symonds

Rule No.2: No Questions

Copyright © 2022 to Mel Symonds

http://www.melsymonds.co.uk/

This is a work of fiction. Although actual places are used in some
cases, all characters and happenings are fabricated.

Editing and formatting by Amanda:
www.letsgetbooked.com

Cover illustrated by Vicky Long

ISBN: 978-1-3999-2072-8

For Vera and Edith, please keep asking questions...

# chapter One

## A can of worms

"Clara, I think you're bored," says Reggie, standing next to me on the green wooden platform of the climbing frame in our school playground.

I watch him turn and leap towards the first monkey bar. "Bored?" I question. "No, trust me, Tammy and Charlotte are acting suspicious and are definitely up to something."

"Why?" he asks, as he swings away from me.

"Because they are both mean and horrid," replies

Bella, who is already on the blue wooden platform ahead of Reggie and is now about to climb down the metal pole.

Reggie laughs. "Well, yes, we all know that!" With a giant swing, he jumps from the last monkey bar and successfully lands next to Bella. "I mean, what are they doing to make you so suspicious this time, Clara?"

Standing as close to the edge of the wooden ledge as I can, I reach forwards to grab the first monkey bar and get ready to swing towards Reggie. "They are up to something, I just know it," I reply.

How can I explain it to my friends?

It feels like every time I walk near Tammy and Charlotte, they immediately stop talking. Or, I have a strange feeling that I'm being watched, so I look up and then I see them acting like they haven't just been watching me. Like the other day in the school canteen! I was eating sausages and gravy with heaps of mash potato and peas all mixed together, and I looked over to see them both quickly turn away from looking right at me. Or there was that time during maths when they were both pretending to be working really hard, acting like they hadn't just been watching me. THAT was very suspicious, because they NEVER work really hard.

Why are they always watching me?

Well, the simple answer is: They know.

They know that our science teacher, Mrs Elliot, mistakenly shrunk Bella and me to the size of a mouse when we opened her big black bag that she uses to teach us chemistry. They know I saved Bella from Harry-the-Hamster's cage, and that I am the reason Mr Graveshead didn't find a shrunken Bella. Ultimately, they know that Bella and I are the reason he didn't stop our extra science lessons from ever happening ever again!

"They know," I say to Reggie as I slowly move from one monkey bar to the next. "And they want their revenge," I add, while trying to get my breath back.

Reggie reaches his left hand out to grab the start of the net wall. "No, I'm sure you're just being paranoid."

"Huh?" I reply. "Paranoid?"

"You're imagining it," he explains.

"I am not paranoid," I whisper, before quickly looking over my shoulder at the rest of the climbing frame to check that no-one else is listening.

Pausing from climbing the net wall up to the blue twisty slide, Reggie looks across at me and tilts his head to one side. I'm hanging from the last monkey bar that I'm meant to be swinging on, except I'm not moving at all. I decide I can still do this and that jumping down is not an option. I kick out my legs to try and get a swing movement started. If I time this perfectly, I could stretch my foot as far as it will go and reach the platform in front of me.

Reggie shrugs. "Clara, you're bored and you want a new project."

I don't know – Is he right? Am I bored?

I know what Mum would say. That is if she knew anything about Bella and me shrinking to the size of a mouse two months ago. Mum doesn't know though, no way! That's because Mrs Elliot is awesome AND because Bella and I saved the day and we're back to our normal size again. Except I'm 5cm taller. Don't tell Reggie.

Mum would say that this whole situation has opened up 'a can of worms', because that is what she *always* says.

When she says this, I imagine one of those joke baked bean tins full of massive fake multi-coloured inflatable worms. They jump out and explode absolutely everywhere as soon as someone opens it.

Basically, it means that by helping Mrs Elliot and stopping Tammy and Charlotte from ruining our science lesson, it has created a *complicated situation*. A situation where I've realised there is a whole world of people out there that I should be helping and that there is no point sitting around doing nothing.

It is true that in the last two months, Bella, Reggie and I have:

1. Stopped lunchtime athletics club from being cancelled.

Reggie LOVES lunchtime athletics club, but there weren't enough people going to it. So, Bella and I joined and then I got William and Daniel to join too. I spent the whole day begging them both to join and to bring three friends each. Finally, I said I would buy them both any chocolate bar they liked. They ended up really enjoying athletics club and the chocolate bar. Still, with there being more people now going to the club, Mr Knight allowed it to run again.

2. Stopped Mrs Webster from changing the Monday lunch menu from sausages to boiled eggs.

Boiled eggs are not the same as sausages or even vegetarian sausages. I mean boiled eggs? Seriously, come on. We went around trying to get everyone to sign our form to say that they were not happy with this change. So many people signed it, even Tammy and Charlotte! They came straight up to me while Henry was signing his name. Charlotte grabbed the pen off him, signed it, handed it to Tammy so she could sign it, and then Tammy dropped the pen on the floor and walked off – Rude – But at least it was two extra names. It was an epic protest form.

3.	Jumped in to save Neve from walking around all day with a sticker on her back.

Ok, that last one was just me on my own. It really was only a matter of tapping her on the shoulder and asking her if she wanted the sticker (a tooth holding a toothbrush) on her back. She was happy to have it removed and I added it to my sticker collection. That was a good day.

Yes, maybe Reggie is right. I could really do with another project or something to investigate. I keep asking everyone and they all say they're fine. Although, I really do think that there is something strange going on at school at the moment.

"You know what Tammy and Charlotte are like," says Reggie, snapping me out of my daydream. He looks down at me as he climbs the netting and as I continue to hang on the last monkey bar. "I bet they're just trying to annoy you."

"They're up to something," I mumble to myself.

A second attempt at swinging and both my feet are on the blue wooden platform. I am still holding onto the last monkey bar and am trying not to swing back again. Taking a big breath, I dive forwards and quickly grab on to the wooden post. I'm not sure how Bella and Reggie always make it look so easy.

Racing up the net wall, I catch up with Reggie before he pushes himself down the blue twisty slide. "And, the thing is, if they are up to something," I say, stopping him before he goes, "I have a horrible feeling that their plan involves… Mr Netship."

Reggie looks straight at me, his eyes opening wide. "Not Mr Netship," he whispers.

# Chapter Two

## Mr Netship

W ho is Mr Netship? Well, let me tell you all about him.

It all started a week and a half ago, the first week back to school after the Easter holidays. Our teacher, Mr Graveshead, sat at the front of the class on Tuesday morning looking glum. More glum than usual. Staring at the three large piles of papers on the desk in front of him, he took a big breath, his head falling forwards and his black sweaty hair going with it. I watched him as he sat there – something wasn't right.

"Miss. Hornsey," he suddenly announced very loudly, talking about our head teacher at Green Grove School, "had an accident on a boat in Malta. She is fine, all fine, but while she rests and recovers, we have a new acting head teacher."

Mr Netship.

What can I say about Mr Netship? He's long. He looks like his whole body has been stretched, and then at the top of his head is some short, blonde hair. His face... well, he looks like it would be hard for him to smile. When he entered our classroom, there was an icy breeze that followed him. We could all feel it. In one quick shiver, the whole class went as quiet as a library at closing time. He didn't say much, but then he didn't need to. We all knew instantly that he was not the cheery Miss Hornsey that we knew. The Miss Hornsey who would stand smiling at the school gates ready to say, 'Morning, Clara' as I walked through. He did not look like he would smile at me as I walked through the gates, and if he did smile, it might be more terrifying than if he didn't.

It was straight after we met Mr Netship that I saw Tammy and Charlotte coming out of his temporary office. They both had creepy, smug grins on their faces. As soon as they saw me, they both grew 3cm taller and those creepy, smug grins spread wider and became creepier.

The next day, I noticed Mr Netship watching us.

At first, I would see him standing in a doorway or at the end of a corridor, or in the corner of the canteen during lunch. At break, I'd walk over to my favourite red bench, turn to sit down next to Reggie and Bella, and I would see him through a window looking straight at us.

Then, suddenly, he started to appear from nowhere, as if by magic. One second there was a space, and the next second, he'd be in that space. I'm about to say something to Bella in the lunch queue, turn around and he's there with a tray and a plate full of spaghetti. Or I stand up from tying my shoelace, and he's standing there, asking me where I should be and why

I'm not there already.

*** 

"Mr Netship is everywhere," I say to Bella at lunchtime. We're sitting on my favourite red bench in the school playground, ready for our daily planning meeting, and I can see him once again at the window watching us. I try to speak to Bella without moving my mouth because I'm starting to suspect he can lipread. It was on a show I watched, 'The Science of Us'. Lipreading's a way of understanding what someone's saying by looking at the movements of the lips, face, and tongue when there's no sound. It's a skill. A skill that I think Mr Netship has.

"He's what?" shouts Bella.

I sigh, half roll my eyes and put my hand in front of my mouth as if I'm about to yawn. "Bella, I'm saying that Mr Netship is everywhere. Everywhere we go, he's watching us—"

"I'm more concerned about those three over there with the clipboards," she mumbles, staring out across the playground.

"I think he can lipread too," I say, continuing my thoughts while trying not to look at him at the window watching us. I don't know where to look. I look up at the sky so he doesn't suspect that we're talking about him. Then, because that's hurting my neck and probably looks a bit odd, I watch Year 2 having their go on the climbing frame. Yes, that's better. He won't suspect we're talking about him now. "Plus, I saw Tammy and Charlotte come out of his office *again* this morning. I have never seen them look so happy with themselves... or happy to be at school... or just generally happy. I mean, what are they up to?"

"Mer-hal?" Bella says slowly.

"What?"

"Mer-hal..."

"You've lost me."

"I'm trying to read what it says on the back of those clipboards."

Looking over to where Bella has fixed her eyes, and I can see what she means. There are two women and one man looking up at the school. They're standing on the other side of the playground from us on the path that leads up to the main gates. She's wrong though, it's only the man who has the clipboard, the two women have iPads and one of them is pointing it up at the school.

"She's taking a photo," I whisper.

"Oh yes, she is."

"Could be nothing…"

"I recognise them," continues Bella. "Yes, they're the ones I saw after school on Friday standing by the gates as I got into Mum's car."

"Oh…"

"I think they were waiting for everyone to leave," she adds.

"*Merihal*," I say, as we both continue to stare at the strangers. "It says Merihal on the back of his clipboard."

"Merihal, that's interesting," she ponders, still looking over at them. "The question is," she says slowly, "what are they doing and why?"

"THE SCHOOL needs some REPAIRS," bellows a loud, deep voice right next to where we are sitting, jumping me high in the air.

It's Mr Netship.

At the sound of his unexpected and sudden appearance, my bottom actually leaves the bench beneath me! At the same time, my legs kick out and my arms look like I'm trying to swim backstroke. As I fall back down to earth, it feels like my heart knocks into my lungs, sending it on rapid-fire beat mode while I try to breathe.

"Oh, I see," replies Bella calmly, completely unphased by him standing right next to us.

How on earth did he get there without us noticing?! With my heart still on rapid-fire beat mode, I look over to the window where he was standing just a few seconds ago. You know, just in case there are two of him. No, I can't see anyone.

"It seems that you and Clara have a lot of time on your hands this break-time," he says. "Perhaps you should think about joining another club like your friend, Reggie. More clubs would certainly keep you both out of, shall we say, *trouble*." His dark blue eyes dart towards me when he says the word 'trouble' before darting back to Bella again.

Now, there is silence.

I still can't breathe.

My mouth is completely dry, like a cactus in the middle of a desert, and my lungs have forgotten their main job.

"Or do you have more questions you'd like to ask?" he eventually says.

Questions!

Did he say, '*more questions*'?

No, you NEVER ask a teacher a question. It's a trick. Every. Single. Time. Don't fall for it. It is my very important and much needed crucial rule – Rule Number Two: No Questions!

Every time a teacher says, '*Do you have any questions*', they don't really mean it. What they are actually saying is, '*I have given you all the information you need to carry on working in silence and if you ask me any questions, it means you weren't listening to anything I have been saying up to this point.'* If you fall for 'the trick' and ask them a question, then the only answer you will get is a cryptic question in return, like, *'Well, you tell me, Clara?'*

No. Absolutely no questions. I am NEVER falling for that trick again. Plus, let's be honest here, if no-one else in the room looks like they are about to ask a question, isn't it just easier to search the internet when you get home? Way too much attention and way too many chances for eye rolls or big tuts and sighs. Or worse – standing up in front of the class and spending the next twenty minutes trying to answer the question you just asked the teacher.

*'Do you have any questions?'* they ask.

No Questions.

In the corner of my brain there is a big red flashing light to remind me not to fall for *'the trick'*. The red flashing light spins and turns like a tall lighthouse on the edge of a cliff, warning boats out at sea that they are getting way too close to rocks.

If it's really bad, like now with Mr Netship, then there is also a really loud alarm that shouts out, 'IT'S A TRICK!' every three seconds, just in case. No good would come from asking Mr Netship a question. That can ONLY be bad.

While trying to control my heart from jumping straight out of my chest AND reminding my lungs that it is their job to provide my body with oxygen, I look at Bella. She is still looking at the three people on the other side of the playground, her mouth twitching and her eyebrows closing in on each other.

*Is she about to ask a question?*

My red flashing warning light in my head is spinning around and this is not helping me to control my heartbeat. "No," I croak through my dry mouth. "Nothing, no, just no, nothing no," I manage to say.

"GOOD!" Mr Netship bellows. "Then how about you both get up and go and *do* something before break finishes?"

"Yes, of course," I mumble, as Mr Netship quickly turns away from us. With four strides, he is half way across the playground, marching straight towards the strangers.

"That was weird," Bella whispers.

As we watch Mr Netship greet the strangers with a firm handshake and nodding head, the alarm in my head stops flashing. That was a completely scary crazy situation!

Something *is* going on.

Tammy and Charlotte are up to something and Mr Netship is up to something. Yes, there are definitely some weird things going on at school at the moment.

# Chapter Three

## Standing On Our Stage

At Green Grove School, we have this wooden stage that moves on wheels. When we see it, it's a sign to stop feeling down that the summer holidays are over and be happy, because rehearsals for the Christmas school play are about to begin. Other than this, the stage is magically hidden and never to be seen for the rest of the year.

It's April. I'm sitting on the floor in the hall, waiting for the school assembly to start, and I'm trying to be quiet. Mr Graveshead has said to stop talking twice but then a minute goes by and Bella will say something, and it would be rude not to reply to her. This time though, I don't reply because a strange squeaking sound has made me completely forget what I was about to say to her.

*WEE-EEE-EEE-EEE, WEE-EEE-EEE-EEE*

It is coming from the corner of the room. Bella can hear it too – her head turns towards the noise and her eyes dart over the heads sitting in front of us. As the noise gets louder and closer, Mr Ball and Miss Tully's bottoms burst through the double doors at the side of the room. At that moment, the whole entire school remembers at exactly the same time to be completely and utterly quiet as we watch those bottoms.

*WEE-EEE-EEE-EEE*

The rest of their bodies appear through the doors, bent over, pulling something into the room. A foot appears. Two feet with legs connected to a long body, and it is standing on top of our Christmas stage!

*WEE-EEE-EEE-EEE*

It's April.

*WEE-EEE-EEE-EEE*

The Christmas stage is still moving across the room. Mr Ball and Miss Tully are pulling it along and then at the other end, Mrs Regan and Mr Rutt have appeared through the doors pushing the stage.

*WEE-EEE-EEE-EEE*

Standing with his hands on his hips, on top of our Christmas stage, is the long body of Mr Netship.

"Stop here," he announces.

I'm shocked. I'm not sure if I should laugh or if I should cry. Instead, I just stare at him.

It's April.

I keep reminding myself it's only April as my confused emotions absorb Mr Netship standing on my beloved Christmas stage with two teachers on either side of him. He is still standing very straight with his hands on his hips, while the other four teachers are bent over and breathing very heavily. I have never before seen our Christmas stage being used for an assembly. Plus, I have never ever seen someone standing on top of it while it's being moved. When

Miss Hornsey is here, she simply walks into the hall and stands at the front of the room with both feet on the floor.

"Good morning, Green Grove School!" he shouts out to us all.

A dark, heavy silence fills the room as we all stare at him in disbelief. I'm not sure I've ever heard the whole school so quiet before.

"Good morning, Mr Netship," the teachers in the room suddenly shout out, with some of the more alert children joining in half way through, which sounds like an echo on the end of the sentence.

"I have some great news for you all!" he announces, his arms open wide as his voice booms around the room.

With a dramatic pause, he brings his hands together in front of him. And then, as if he has just thought of something, he attempts to smile. The full teeth-bearing strain on his face sends a ripple of gasps throughout the room. He does look scary. I'm so glad I'm sitting far away from him, near the back of the room. I feel sorry for those poor kids at the front. I want to look at Bella and Reggie on my left, but even at this safe distance, I know better than to turn my head from facing forwards.

"Next Monday, each and every one of you will be on a school trip to 'BioZone', a revolutionary environmental company."

Everyone? The whole school on the same trip together? That's seven classes of thirty children all going to the exact same place on the exact same day? 210 of us! That has *never* been done before. Usually, Miss Hornsey splits it between a few weeks, with the Reception Class, Year 1 and Year 2 going one week and the rest of us going on another week.

And we are all going *next Monday*? That is very soon.

I can't move my head to look at Bella to see if she's doing her 'wrinkled forehead look', which makes her look like she's trying to solve a five-lined maths question. I bet she is though because THIS is confusing.

"It will be a chance for this school to look into the new ways of protecting our planet that are being developed there," he continues, and I realise I haven't been listening to a word he has been saying. "Any questions?" he adds.

Not one single hand goes up to ask a question – of course there are no questions.

"One last thing – There will be some new faces walking around the school this week. Nothing to concern yourselves with. Do not approach them and do not ask them any questions."

I swear he just looked directly at Bella when he said '*do not ask them any questions*'.

"That will be all!" he shouts.

As if this strange assembly hasn't been odd enough already, Mr Netship glances at the four teachers at his side and clicks his fingers. The four teachers inch forward, move to their positions on either side of the stage, and Mr Netship then places his fists firmly on his hips and stares out at the back of the room. It's like he's turned into a statue of himself.

"What is he doing?" I whisper to myself, as I watch in amazement as they wheel him out again. Miss Hornsey doesn't do this, she just walks out the room.

***

"A whole school trip next Monday," Bella ponders aloud as soon as the squeaking sound has got far enough away that we can hear her. "Mr Netship is becoming more and more suspicious."

"I know," I whisper, getting up from sitting on the floor and slowly following our class back out of the hall. "It's so soon."

"Do you know what else is weird?" continues Bella to Reggie and me as we start to walk down the corridor. "Mum said that company 'Merihal' is a property development company – they just build houses!"

"Really?" I ask.

"And loads of them, too. Mum said they try to squeeze loads of houses into tiny spaces."

Looking down at my feet as I walk, I add this new

bit of information to my list of strange things going on at this school. "That's odd."

"Yeah… they are trying to build loads of houses on some old farmland near Mum's work."

"But BioZone sounds AMAZING!" cuts in Reggie, jumping on the first stair up to our classroom. "I honestly cannot wait."

"Erm, yes," I reply, shuffling up the stairs behind him. I didn't listen to the assembly, but if Reggie says it sounds amazing, then maybe this trip isn't such a bad thing.

"It sounds *too* good!" exclaims Bella, marching up the last of the stairs. "A whole school trip suddenly out of the blue like this?!" she questions, turning to face me as I reach the top of the stairs too.

"I know," I reply, slowly shaking my head, "something isn't right."

Watching Bella march towards our classroom, her brown curly hair jumps up and down behind her. She reaches the door ahead of us and suddenly turns. Her forehead is creased and her lips are pushed tightly together. "It feels like Mr Netship wants us all out of the way… So, I'm going to ask Mr Graveshead."

I can't believe my ears. "What? Ask him what?!"

"Why are we all going to BioZone on the same day? Why has the school never attempted a whole school trip like this in the past? How is this place relevant to every class in this school? Why wouldn't it be easier to split it between two or three days or even weeks?"

"That sounds like a lot of questions," Reggie laughs, stepping past Bella and making his way to his seat.

"Too many!" I say, feeling horrified by what she is about to do. Watching Bella walk off to her seat too, I quickly catch them both up and jump in front of them. "Are you *seriously* going to ask Mr Graveshead all those questions? We don't ask teachers questions!"

Bella sighs. "Not this again."

"Why not?" asks Reggie.

"Because the only answer you will get will be something like, erm… *'Don't you want to go, Bella?'*" I say in my best grumpy Mr Graveshead voice. "You know the teachers never answer a question without asking another question in return."

"Clara, you're wrong," replies Bella. "This is the *only* way we'll find out what is going on."

"Trust me," I whisper as Mr Graveshead enters the room and we all sit down in our seats, "there has to be another way. Nothing good has ever come from asking a teacher a question."

Bella looks at me with a half eye roll, tilts her head to the side, sighs and then puts her hand straight up in the air. Oh no, my feet feel prickly and my left leg can't stop jiggling on the spot.

"Right," shouts Mr Graveshead, because he always shouts. "There are some maths questions on the board, which you should know how to work out the answers to because we looked at this last lesson… Bella, you have a question?"

"May I ask a question about the assembly?"

"Do you need to ask me now?"

Typical! Questions being answered with more questions. I sink in my chair as my left leg goes into hyper-jiggling mode. Next thing that will happen is that she'll be asked to replay the whole assembly again until she finds the answer to her own question.

"Yes, I do."

"Well, umm, what it is?"

"Yes, *I* would like to know what your *question* is too," says a loud, deep voice from the other side of the room.

It's Mr Netship… AGAIN. He has suddenly appeared in our classroom and is standing by William's chair. Where did he come from? How long has he been there? Is there a series of secret corridors in our school, which means he can suddenly be anywhere in seconds? Perhaps he's installed cameras and secret listening devices, too.

*Don't ask the question,* I try to tell Bella telepathically through my bulging eyes. *Time to back down and pretend you don't really have a question.*

Telepathy – I have seen superheroes do this all the time, especially the X-Men. They talk to each other through thoughts in their heads and have entire conversations without anyone else knowing anything about it. This would be a great time for Bella and me to realise that we have such powers.

*Do not ask the question Bella!* I shout through my bulging eyes, hoping that there are some telepathic sound waves radiating from my brain and going straight into her brain. *Abort. Abort.*

"I was just wondering—"

*No, Bella, it's a trick!* I try again.

My red flashing warning light in my head is back, and the 'IT'S A TRICK' alarm is also sounding out. Can she not hear it too?

"Why is the whole school on the same trip together? Why are we not going on different days?"

"I seeeeeeeee," Mr Netship replies slowly, his eyes on Bella, moving to Reggie and then to me.

As he looks at me, I freeze. My jiggling left leg freezes too. It still wants to move but it can't – it just thinks it's moving. Can he read minds? Did he get my telepathic thoughts instead of Bella?

"Don't you *want* to go on this trip?" he asks her.

I KNEW he would say that. I just knew it.

"Um, yes, I—" she starts to reply.

"I would have thought that a *star* pupil in science, such as yourself, would be delighted to go on such a trip to BioZone. Is it not a place that sounds *interesting* to you?"

"Yes, it is, I just—"

"GOOD!" he shouts, interrupting her again before she can say anything more. "Then perhaps it is that you question what is *best* for this school? Perhaps you were in the meeting when this trip was arranged? No, you were not. So, I think you should listen to Mr Graveshead now and the maths work he has set for you to do... And do not worry about your questions, Bella," he adds in a softer voice after a small but deadly pause. "Because I suspect you have *lots* and *lots* of things you would like to ask, so, yes, this class can be in *my* group for the school trip."

What?! What did he just say? Did he just say that we have an entire day with him in our group? No! Mr Whitehead usually comes in and joins our class on school trips. He's great. He laughs, and he chats to us while Mr Graveshead mutters and shouts. This cannot be happening!

As I sink into my seat, wondering if this day could possibly get any worse, Bella sinks into her seat too, with her ears stopping at her shoulders. She asked a question. She asked Mr Netship of all people. No good ever comes from asking questions.

Looking up from staring at the table in front of me, my eyes catch a smirk on the corners of Mr Netship's mouth. Turning to leave, his eyes scan the faces in the room before they stop at Tammy and Charlotte. Then he quickly nods at them both. I saw it, I definitely saw it and they did too. They catch the nod and a slow smirk appears on their mouths. I shiver at the sight of it and it runs all the way down my back. Well, that proves it – I'm not being paranoid. They are up to something and it involves Mr Netship.

# Chapter Four

## And So It Begins

Standing at the very back of the queue to get on the coach, Bella lifts her head from staring at the ground. "I am really sorry," she says.

"We know," replies Reggie with a cheerful tune to his words. He has a slight bounce to his step too. I look at him quizzically. It's early. No-one else looks as cheerful as he does this early in the morning. Henry, who's in front of Reggie, looks like he forgot to brush his hair and has not stopped yawning. Then, Charlie, in front of Henry, looks like he could actually still be asleep.

"I'm just really sorry we have Mr Netship all day today because of me," she mumbles, kicking the ground as she does so.

Bella has been saying '*I'm sorry*' all week. Reggie always answers the same, '*we know*' but as the week went on it sounded faded and automatic. Every time she says it, I can't reply to her as a big lump gets stuck in my throat. I stay quiet and nod or just smile at her. This time, though, I clap my hands together.

"Bella, it's going to be OK," I say.

"OK? It's going to be brilliant!" shrieks Reggie, spinning round to face us both. "BioZone is cutting edge! It's a complete game-changer," he sings.

When Reggie finishes his loud and sudden interruption, I stare at him and he stares back. His head is still moving side to side and his eyes are slowly getting bigger and bigger. I'm not sure if he's wanting me to say something.

"Telepathy doesn't work," I say aloud, wondering if maybe he is actually now trying to talk to me through his thoughts. "Well, it might do. Perhaps we just need a bit more practice... No, sorry, I can't hear anything."

"What?!" he replies. Turning back round, he quickly catches up with the queue, muttering to himself. I'm sure I can hear him say something about us 'not getting it'.

"Look," I say, turning back to face Bella again. "It's going to be OK," I repeat. "It's annoying that *Boatman* is in our group, and it would be more fun without him, but we won't let it get to us."

"Yes, right, *Boatman*, of course," Bella mumbles.

We have started calling Mr Netship '*Boatman*'. It came to me on Friday when I saw him standing at the window *again* during break-time and Bella and I were talking about him. With Mr Netship possibly a skilled lipreader and Tammy and Charlotte spying on us, we can't risk using his real name.

So, Mr Netship is now called '*Boatman*'. Get it? Net-ship. Ship: A type of boat. Plus, a Boatman is also a bug – a Lesser Water Boatman. A bug found in water with two long legs. Perfect. Charlotte and Tammy are called '*those two*'. I wasn't very happy with their new nickname. That was Bella's choice.

Once Reggie had joined us on our bench, and Bella had said she was sorry, again, we discussed how '*those two*' and '*Boatman*' were obviously spying on us for some reason.

"Those two were standing there watching me when I came in late this morning," Reggie had told us. "I mean, I was only a little bit late because my shoelace came undone, but as soon as they saw me, they went straight off to his office."

In conclusion, we decided we needed to work out what was going on, but it was probably safer to meet up at the weekend without all these spies and lipreaders constantly watching us.

"We're going to enjoy this school trip today," I continue, as Bella and I shuffle our feet along in the queue for the coach. "And," I add in a whisper as we get closer to the door. "We're also going to find out what Boatman is up to."

That's our plan.

By the time we had moved from the zip slide, to the net frame and then to the swings in the park on Saturday, we had formulated a plan: We are going to let 'Boatman' and 'those two' think that we don't know they are watching us, but really, we are watching them. Mr Netship is definitely suspicious, and well, Tammy and Charlotte are always suspicious.

"Did you find out anything more about Merihal?" asks Bella, looking a bit happier.

"Well," I whisper, tapping Reggie on the shoulder and getting him to join us too. "I had a look on the internet and I couldn't find any mention of a company called 'Merihal' that do 'school building repairs'. There's a Rock Band called Merihal that raised money for a school's building repairs... Oh and a boat in Cornwall."

"Oh!" says Reggie, his forehead wrinkling.

"But," I continue. "When I searched 'Merihal property development', there were loads of results! No website for the company, just small newspaper articles investigating them and pages of complaints!"

Reggie raises his eyebrows high into his forehead. "Complaints?" he questions. "Did you read them?"

"Oh yeah, and they sounded awful! There were things on the houses falling apart and crumbling, and garden walls falling down. There was lots about flooding because of drainage issues that were ignored, and then there was also something about sewage problems."

"Ewwwwwww!" cuts in Bella.

"Yeah, that one sounded quite stinky! But that's not all," I whisper, beckoning them both to lean in. "There was one newspaper that said Merihal was constantly building on land before they were legally allowed to, and something about them getting hold of land that wasn't even for sale."

"No way!" exclaims Reggie, standing there in shock before realising the queue to get on the coach has moved.

As Reggie runs to catch up with Henry, I turn to Bella. "Why would a dodgy housing development company be doing building repairs to our school?

Very suspicious!"

"I don't know, but we're going to find out," says Bella. "Plus, it doesn't sound like they are going to be very good *repairs* if all those complaints about them are true."

As I climb the four steep steps to get on the coach, I'm feeling happier about our plan. I want to spin round to face Bella with a big smile with two thumbs up, but as I reach the top of the stairs, my smile drops to the floor. Tammy and Charlotte are sitting right at the front of the coach. They are both looking right at me with identical long thin smiles that stretch across their faces. Next to them, on the other side of the aisle, is Mr Netship, looking down at his phone. Behind him is Reggie, sitting next to Daniel. There are two free seats directly behind Tammy and Charlotte. Quickly, I look ahead at the back of the coach for any other free seats.

"Clara and Bella, you can sit there," bellows Mr Netship, pointing to the seats that I do not want to sit on. He doesn't even look up from his phone.

"Right behind us," says Charlotte in her fake kind voice. It's the voice that sends a shiver down my spine.

'*I am so sorry,*' I can imagine Bella saying from behind me. Or maybe she actually said it through telepathy.

# Chapter Five

## Welcome to BioZone

I can see the BioZone buildings miles before we actually get to them. Three huge white cylinders in the distance of absolutely nowhere but trees, green fields and the road our coach is on. Looking out of my window, the blue words 'BioZone' appear on the edge of the green horizon on the top of the middle cylinder. The rest of the buildings slowly appear the closer we get to our turning off the road. Once past the buildings, the coach swings off the fast road, circles us left and left again. Then it's right, over

two roundabouts, and I can see more smaller ⬛
buildings. All the buildings are connected to form ⬛
shape with the three huge cylinders in the middle.

"Cuuuuutttttttttting-edge," sings Reggie with his
arms open wide as he jumps down the stairs and off
the coach behind Bella and me.

It is a bright sunny day, and apart from the large
white buildings, everything looks very green. Lots of
green trees, green bushes and green grass on either
side of the grey car park we're standing in. The whole
thing looks friendly and relaxing and like the start of a
holiday after a really long journey.

"Look at this place!" exclaims Reggie, spinning
around slowly. "I honestly can't wait."

I smile back at him and clear my throat with a
cough. It's not that I want to say anything, it's just that
for the last forty-five minutes, Bella and I have been
completely silent as we sat on the coach. We
communicated through the fingerspelling alphabet
sign language that Miss Tully taught us last year.
Fingerspelling is an awesome way of spelling out every

your hands. It's very useful. We ̩ we've been told to stop talking in it when we want to talk about ...̫ʟ̩̩g, but my big brother Darren is there. He's so unbelievably annoying and will listen and snigger at anything we say. Today, though, it was an excellent thing to know while sitting on a coach with two spies sitting in front of us that would tell Mr Netship everything we said.

"Welcome to BioZone!" a woman shouts out, causing me to turn around from facing Reggie. The woman has a huge smile on her face that instantly makes me want to smile back and listen to her. She has very short black hair, big round glasses and I like her dark green dress with large yellow triangles on it. "I'm Mali. You are our Red Group today and we will be starting out in Conference Room B, where we will introduce you to what we do here at BioZone. From here, we will have a quick break before a tour through our labs. Then after lunch, there will be lots of activities and fun practical experiments for you all to try out."

Reggie is jumping up and down next to me. I don't think he can help it. Plus, he doesn't seem to notice the stern looks from Mr Netship, who is obviously irritated with all the jumping.

*'This is going to be fun,'* I fingerspell sign language to Bella while Reggie is distracting Mr Netship. I forget to do the 'h' in *'this'* and the 'g' at the beginning of *'going'* but I finish it with two big thumbs up and a huge smile, so she knows what I'm saying.

"We'll just wait for Blue Group to set off," says Mali, meaning Year 6, who have started walking away from their coach. "And then we will head in this direction." She points to a grey path with small neat green bushes on either side. I can see Year 6 crossing in front of it and heading toward a completely different path.

In amongst the chatty Year 6 group, I see Mrs Elliot and my heart drops into my stomach. They are so lucky. It would be so cool to have Mrs Elliot in our group on this school trip instead of Mr Netship. My face must show my sadness because when she sees me, she smiles and winks, screwing up her whole face as she does so. Stopping before the path takes her behind a large tree, Mrs Elliot looks at me exactly like Mum does when she says goodbye at the start of a new school year after weeks of summer holidays together. I smile back at Mrs Elliot with my best and practiced '*I'm fine*' face, even though I'm not really.

"Hope you have *fun* today, Bella," says a familiar singsong voice behind me.

I turn and my smile fades – Tammy and Charlotte are walking in circles around Bella.

"Yeah, hope you have a *fun day*," laughs Tammy.

This is odd. OK, their emphasis on the word 'fun' is really odd and annoying, but it's the talking to us that's odd. Usually, they don't come near us. Since our shrunken adventure, Tammy and Charlotte have kept their distance from us. Yes, they are clearly up to something and have been spying on us, but they don't usually *say* anything. It seems with Mr Netship as acting head teacher, everything is changing again.

I instinctively look over at him, and he quickly

flicks his head away as if he hasn't been watching us and he hasn't seen what's going on.

"I'm sure it will be *fun*!" Bella replies in her best 'I'm bored of talking to you' voice. "BioZone sounds amazing, so how could it be anything but *fun?*"

"HA HA HA HA!" screams Tammy, which makes me jump because it was very loud and sudden and fake-sounding but most definitely loud.

Stopping and standing directly in front of Bella, Charlotte crosses her arms. "Well, let's hope that it is, and that nothing *goes wrong* today."

Bella looks at her and her forehead wrinkles. "Why would anything go wrong?"

"Oh, I don't know, sometimes things go wrong and... Well, we just wouldn't want anything to happen or anyone to get expelled from school or anything... You know... Would we?"

"Hey, what is your problem?" Reggie steps in as Bella and Charlotte start a completely no-blinking staring competition.

"Nothing. I'm just saying," says Charlotte, not

blinking.

"Well, maybe you should say it somewhere else," replies Bella, still staring straight back at her.

Opening her mouth to reply, Charlotte is interrupted.

"OK, let's go!" shouts Mali, waving her hand in the air. "Follow me to Conference Room B!"

With the signal to move, the great wave of Year 5 class breaks the stare between Charlotte and Bella as they push and weave amongst us. We head for the narrow grey path next to the building with neat green bushes on either side. Moving along with the rest of Year 5, we drift as far as we can away from Tammy and Charlotte.

On the path, I look behind me. Tammy and Charlotte are at the back of the line chatting to each other. Tammy has her hands all over her brown hair, twisting a big handful of it around her hand while Charlotte watches her, shaking her head. At the beginning of the line ahead of us, Mr Netship is chatting away to Mr Graveshead. Mr Graveshead is looking at him and nodding. He has a weird smile on his face. Actually, that might be his normal smile, it just looks weird because I'm not used to seeing him smile.

I turn to Reggie, who's walking next to me. "That was odd with Those Two."

"I guess so," he replies with a shrug. "I don't think they want to be here. I think they're looking for trouble and they want to annoy us. You know what they're like."

"Yeah, but it was weird when they said about something *going wrong* today."

Reggie looks at me and wrinkles his nose. "I'm hoping that's just them being mean and horrid."

"Hopefully… Hey, you and Daniel weren't saying much on the coach."

"No, he had his cards with him, so we were playing that. But," he adds, leaning in close. "I wasn't too busy playing cards that I didn't notice '*Merihal*' on Boatman's phone."

"Really, a message?"

"Yep."

"What did it say?"

"It said, 'We're here'."

"We're here," I repeat, "and anything else?"

"Nothing from them, no. Boatman sent a message back to them. It said: 'Good. Let me know if you have any issues.'"

"Oh, *issues*, right," I reply, really wanting there to be more in the messages than just that.

"Then he spent the rest of the journey looking at houses on beaches."

"What?"

"You know, like somewhere you might go on holiday, like Greece. Yeah, blue sea, sandy beaches and blue sky. He was looking at houses and they were all right next to beaches."

"Oh, right... I see..."

"I'd better tell Bella," says Reggie, stepping forward and tapping her on the shoulder.

So, Merihal are at our school today and Mr Netship is looking at holiday houses by the sea. I listen to the sounds of Bella gasping and wonder if this really is suspicious. It could simply be a building company helping out with repairs to a school and Mr Netship planning a holiday. What repairs though and why them?

As I leave Reggie and Bella to whisper their own ideas to each other, a feeling of doom creeps over me. It's like that feeling I get when I spot a dark cloud in the corner of a clear blue sky. Or it's the realisation that a teacher is saying my name and I don't know how long they have been saying it for because I've been in the middle of an awesome daydream. It's a feeling that my happiness is about to be ruined. Unconsciously, I look over my shoulder and immediately see the source of the doom: Tammy and Charlotte are both standing really close behind me with long, thin smiles.

Slowly turning my head back, I reach my hand out to grab Reggie's arm to stop him talking or saying any more to Bella.

"Don't you think, Clara?" he says, turning towards me before looking behind me. The happy look on his face disappears as he spots Tammy and Charlotte. Like he's suddenly noticed a big splodge of gravy on his favourite t-shirt.

How long have they been there and what did they hear?

Obviously, they have been standing there long enough, because the next thing I feel is a painful barge to my shoulder as they both walk through the middle of us. They walk past the shocked faces of Reggie and Bella, through the unsuspecting shoulders of Daniel and Henry, and all the way to the front of the line. With a ripple of annoyance from all the shoulders they have barged through, Charlotte reaches Mr Netship. As she reaches him, he leans to one side so she can whisper in his ear while he walks. Standing up straight, he doesn't turn around, but Charlotte does, and she looks straight at me, raising one eyebrow and squashing her lips together.

# chapter six

## A Quick Exit

Conference Room B is like walking into a cinema. There is a huge screen on the stage to the left of me at the front of the room and rows of black seats to my right. Every row of seating is one step higher than the last row until the very back of the room. In the middle of the rows of seats are bright red steps taking you all the way to the top. The last row looks so high that the seats actually look down at the stage. That has *got* to be the best place to sit.

With my foot on the first bright red step and my

mind ready to run all the way to the top, something falls down in front of me. It is a long arm covered in a dark blue jumper.

"*You* can sit there," says Mr Netship, pointing to a seat in the fourth row.

*There? What? Why?* I grumble but completely and utterly to myself and inside my head. There is no way I am going to *ask him* why I have to sit so close to the front when everyone else gets to go wherever they want!

Slumping down in the seat next to Bella, we look at each other before turning to watch Mr Netship. He strolls across the room, his long legs taking three slow strides before he's exactly where he wants to sit. I can hear the rest of Year 5 choose exactly the seat they want too. Most of them run all the way to the top of the stairs. My eyes narrow as I look at him.

"Don't let him get to you," whispers Bella. "We'll find out what he's up to."

I'm about to agree with her but add, 'Before meeting Boatman, I thought Mr Graveshead was bad', when the lights in the room dim. With this, the loud noises of everyone finding a seat and then changing their minds, stops and the room quietens. The screen in front of us lights up and the words 'BioZone' appear in blue letters. Getting comfortable in the big seats, I watch as the screen then flashes to a man standing outside in a field. He has silver hair, which matches his silver glasses, light blue eyes, a big smile on his face and very white teeth. The field all around him has long, bright green grass, and the sky is completely blue.

"Carbon dioxide is all around us," he says, looking straight at the camera. "In fact, if it wasn't for carbon dioxide, then the Earth's oceans would freeze. It is a greenhouse gas that traps heat close to the Earth, which is good for life on our planet. However, too much carbon dioxide causes problems."

I like watching films. I could really do with some crisps or popcorn though, and maybe an orange juice.

Glancing over the heads in front of me, I see Reggie and I laugh to myself. He grabbed a front-row seat as soon as we entered the room. He doesn't seem to care that there are really high seats behind him. Reggie also doesn't seem to care about Mr Netship's constant stern looks at him and he certainly isn't going to let him spoil his fun. I should have looked this place up on the internet before we came like Reggie told me to.

"Changes are happening faster," the man on the film continues. "Changes in where and how plants grow, changes in the sea and changes in entire ecosystems like tropical rainforests."

Switching location, the screen flies over the top of a massive rainforest. Swooping down and up again, it whizzes past it, showing how massive the forest is. "Once carbon dioxide is added to the atmosphere, it stays for a very, very long time. In fact, it stays between 300 to 1,000 years—"

"That is a long time," I mutter to Bella.

"Huh?"

"Carbon dioxide… Are you watching the film?"

"I've seen it already," she replies. "It's on their website. I've watched it like three times… Hey, look at

Boatman. What's he up to?"

Looking over at where Mr Netship is sitting, at the end of the front row with four seats in-between him and the rest of us, I see he's staring at his phone again. I can't see Mr Graveshead. I think he's probably sitting a few rows behind us and right at the end, where he can watch everyone. I mustn't turn my head and look or he'll shout that I'm not watching the film. That would be completely embarrassing. So, without looking, I'm guessing that he's over my right shoulder and that Tammy and Charlotte are at the back of the room. I saw them run right to the back as soon as we arrived, so they are probably still there. They are so lucky.

"He *keeps* looking at his phone," Bella says, replying to her own question. "He can't still be messaging this Merihal company, can he? Do you think we'll go back and they'll have completely transformed the school?"

I don't reply. It's way too risky to say anything with Mr Graveshead so close behind. He'll shout at me to stop talking and everyone will turn to stare.

"Here at BioZone," continues the man on the film, "we have turned to nature for the answers to the problems that human-beings have created." He's now wearing a long white coat and is walking in-between desks of plants and science-y looking glass things. "And we believe that plants hold the answers."

With the sudden stop of the film, the lights above us slowly get brighter and Mali quietly walks on the stage.

"Right," she says, her voice appearing from every corner of the room. "I hope you enjoyed our video. We're going to have a quick break and then I'm going to run through the key elements of the video before our tour of the labs." She finishes with a smile, opens her hands up, claps them together and then turns to leave.

"That sounds cool," says Bella.

As Mali leaves the stage, the door we originally came in through, to the left of us now, opens and a woman comes in. She is pulling a grey trolley behind her. As she wheels it in to position, I can instantly see that it is full of drinks and snacks and delicious cake-looking things. I think I can see cartons of juice at one end of the trolley, apples and bananas in the middle, and it looks like there may well be packets of crisps and pastries at the other end. They look good. I love pastries, especially a cinnamon bun.

I'm guessing that the whole of Year 5 has spotted what I've seen too because as soon as the woman with the trolley looks over at us, we all move.

"Slowly! One at a time!" Mr Graveshead shouts out behind me as the noise in the room gets louder.

"I need to get to the front of the queue," announces May with urgency. Jumping up from sitting the other side of Bella, she doesn't wait for us to move out of her way. Instead, she climbs over us. I only realise what she's doing when her hand flies through the air and her elbow hits my nose.

"Watch it!" cries Bella, pushing May's foot off her lap.

"I was about to move!" I say, holding my nose and trying to protect my face while May looks at where she's putting her feet.

"You don't understand," she shouts, trying to dive headfirst towards the aisle. "Mum has packed me a brown banana and a packet of mints with my sandwich for lunch."

"I thought you liked bananas," I say, helping her over my seat. May always arrives at school still eating her banana from breakfast. She finishes it and then immediately runs over to the game of football that has started before the school bell goes.

"This banana is brown."

"I hate it when they go brown."

"AND it has completely squashed the sandwich," she says as she dives past me and lands in a kind of handstand into a forward roll manoeuvre. She's now blocking everyone trying to walk down the red stairs. "So, there's bits of brown banana all over my squashed sandwich."

"That's bad," I say, watching her get back on her feet again. I'm quite impressed with her 'dive into handstand into a forward roll manoeuvre', but then I have seen her swinging on a trapeze before. It was hanging from a tree. She then did a double roll on it before a perfect two feet landing. "Is that really all you got in your packed lunch?"

"Ermmm, no… I ate the oat bar on the coach."

I nod. "That makes sense."

As May runs down the stairs, rushing round and past everyone walking, I get up from my seat. While the rest of the room heads over to form a queue for the snack trolley, I turn to watch Mr Netship. I can hear Mr Graveshead shouting about something and trying to control the queue, but Mr Netship is completely not helping him. He looks at Mr Graveshead waving his arms around and then he slowly walks to the right side of the room. It looks like he is going to the back of the queue except he keeps going towards the green exit sign.

"Tammy!" I suddenly hear Mr Graveshead shout. "Stop pushing in."

"I'm not."

"I just saw you with my own eyes! Now go back and

stand behind Peter."

"Boatman is leaving," I whisper to Bella as we join Reggie at the bottom of the stairs.

"I said *behind* Peter!" Mr Graveshead shouts.

"This is so unfair," huffs Tammy.

While everyone else watches Tammy sulking, Reggie, Bella and I watch Mr Netship leave the room through a different door. He has pushed open the exit door, and it has quickly swung shut behind him but not completely closed. The three of us dart over to where he had been standing.

"Right, give me an update," I hear him say.

We're pretending to be at the back of the long snack queue. As it starts to slowly move forwards, I put my foot forward and actually step backwards.

"...Can't you make it look like the building is unsafe?" I think I hear Mr Netship say. The last part of his sentence sounded distant.

"Building unsafe? Is that what he just said?" I whisper to Bella and Reggie, who are also pretending to move forward in the snack queue.

"I think so," replies Reggie. "It's really loud in here."

"He's moved away from the door," says Bella

The argument at the front of the snack queue seems to have sorted itself out, and the line is moving much quicker now. I can see Charlotte and Tammy are getting closer to the front of the queue, with Peter stuck in the middle of them. Poor Peter.

Tammy and Charlotte seem to have forgotten that they are meant to be watching us. Or maybe their acting skills have got *a lot* better.

"He has definitely moved," says Bella, who has stuck her head out through the exit door. "We need to follow him."

I'm not sure I'm ready for this. I mean, I know I want to find out what he is up to, but I'm not sure I'm ready to *actually* follow him so we can carry on listening to his conversation. PLUS, I absolutely cannot believe that Bella just risked sticking her head out the door to see if he has gone. My heart is thumping hard and my hands are shaking a bit. What if someone sees us? What if we get caught?

I look at Mr Graveshead, his arms crossed and his eyes fixed on monitoring the snack trolley, and I glance at Tammy and Charlotte. They still seem to be completely unaware of us standing by the exit door. "OK, let's go," I whisper.

# chapter seven

## The Wrong Way

"Where's he gone?" I whisper to Bella and Reggie.

"I don't know," replies Bella.

Through the exit door of Conference Room B, we have entered the end of a long white corridor. Above us are a row of spotlights lighting the way and at the far end, the corridor splits in two directions.

Reggie looks at me and shrugs his shoulders.

"Come on," urges Bella.

With Bella slightly ahead, we creep down the white corridor, passing white doors with small neat black numbers on them. "Wonder what's in all these rooms," I say before I'm interrupted by a low, deep voice.

"Then we go to Plan B," we hear Mr Netship say, causing the three of us to freeze on-the-spot mid-walk like a game of musical statues. "Did you bring them with you?" he asks.

Bella is the first to move. She carries on creeping forward as Reggie and I stay exactly where we are. As I watch her, I put my hands over my mouth, taking a deep breath at the same time. Reaching the end of the corridor, Bella slowly peeps her head around the corner.

"Good, then put them in the kitchen," says Mr Netship, now sounding a bit further away.

Bella turns to look at Reggie and me. We have still not moved from our frozen mid-walking poses next to door number 18. I'm not sure why I'm still frozen to the spot. I kind of think my brain is getting ready to rush back to Conference Room B. "This way," she whispers, nudging her head to the left.

Walking slowly down this corridor, I notice that it's actually very much like the one we just left. Kind of identical really – The same narrow white corridor with a white ceiling and a grey floor. There are the same white doors with small neat black numbers and a row of spotlights on the ceiling lighting the way.

No sign of Mr Netship, though.

Where is he?

The silence of the empty corridor is scary. I can hear my heart thumping as we walk. I feel like at any moment, Mr Netship is suddenly going to jump out of one of the doors shouting, *'What are you three up to?'*

"Put food down on the floor too," his loud voice booms, knocking me backwards. Even though I was waiting for him to speak, his loud booming voice is like the sound of a trumpet announcing the start of a song! Stopping where I am, I feel like I can't move any further and that my whole body is made of jelly. This is too scary. *'Put food down on the floor.'*

Put them in the kitchen and put food on the floor?

"Not too much food, just scatter it all around a bit,"

Mr Netship continues.

Bella looks back at me, "I can't believe this!" she mouths.

"I know!" I mouth back, placing a shaking hand on top of my beating heart.

Reggie nods at us both to carry on walking, but I'm not sure I want to. I look back at where we have come from as Reggie and Bella tiptoe further down the corridor. Taking a deep breath, I catch up to them.

About half way down this endless corridor, we stumble upon another split. This time we can either continue on or go right.

Mr Netship has gone quiet again.

I look at both Reggie and Bella as we view our options. Reggie shrugs and points to continue down the corridor. I pull my best confused, 'I just don't know' face, then look to my right at the other corridor and try to listen for clues over the sound of my thumping heart. In reply to us both, Bella looks up at the ceiling, sticks her hands out in front of her and stays completely still. She looks very much like a startled meerkat.

"AND," his voices booms out again, causing Bella to dance on the spot as all three of us race to point to the right corridor. "They'll need somewhere that looks like a nest or something."

A nest?

Deciding that his voice is most definitely coming from the right, we creep down the new corridor. This corridor is, again, exactly the same as the other corridors we have already walked down – the spotlights, the doors, the white walls and the grey floor. This time, though, the three of us seem to be tiptoeing along very slowly. I'm kind of letting Reggie and Bella go ahead of me without making it too obvious that I'm scared. I'm moving, just not really moving forward that much.

"You know, a nest," he says, his voice sounding very close even if we still can't see him. "Yes, exactly – make it look like they have been there awhile. Yes. Yes. Perfect!"

While the three of us creep down this new corridor

(seeing the end of it getting closer and noticing that it splits into two), I realise I haven't actually thought this plan out properly. Really, I have just been concerned with finding out what Mr Netship is up to and no further. What *are* we doing? We *will* eventually catch up with him, and then what?

As we reach the split in this corridor, I lean forwards towards Reggie and Bella. "What's the plan?" I whisper.

"We are going to find him and ask him what he is playing at!" Bella whispers, slamming her right fist down on the palm of her left hand.

"What?"

"We are going to say we heard *everything* and that he had better tell us what he is up to."

"Are we?" asks Reggie.

"I thought we were going to—" I say before Mr Netship's voice cuts in again.

"How long do you need?" he says.

"I think he's coming back," whispers Reggie. "He sounds much closer."

"But… I thought," I say again, although I'm not really sure how to finish that sentence.

Peering her head around the corner, Bella quickly looks back at us. "I can see him."

Oh no. Oh no. Oh no. What are we doing? This is bad.

"So, you've got this?" Mr Netship says. "Good. Call me when it's done."

"This is going to be great," whispers Bella, her eyes big and wide. "We can stand right in front of him and ask him what is going on."

"Quickly! We need to run," I say, grasping their arms.

"Clara, what are you doing?" asks Bella.

I'm running back and taking them both with me. This was such a terrible idea! What were we thinking? There is no way we can stand in front of Mr Netship and ask him to tell us what's going on. My red flashing warning light in my head has started up – Bella mustn't ask him a question!

"Are you sure this is the right way?" I hear Reggie

ask as I pull him along. "I think we should have gone left, but you've gone right. Where are we going?"

"Quickly," I whisper, more to myself than to them.

"Clara, we can just ask him what he's up to… Clara, I think we're going the wrong way."

"Bella!" I say in a kind of whisper-shout type way. "There is no way we can *ask* him what he's up to."

"I really don't think we have gone the right way," says Reggie again, slowing down and trying to free his arm from my tight grip. "Plus, I can't hear him anymore and *that* door does not have a sign on it."

Turning around to look at the door behind me, which is the only door at the end of this corridor, I see that Reggie's right – it really doesn't look like the door to Conference Room B. I thought I'd taken us back and ahead of Mr Netship.

All these corridors, they look exactly the same!

I really can't think properly.

Bella mustn't ask Mr Netship any questions! Look what happened the last time she asked him a question. My much-needed Rule Number Two: No Questions.

It's a trick. It's always a trick. No good ever comes from asking questions.

I just need to think and to stop the red flashing light in my head.

"Quickly, get in," I say, opening the door behind me and pulling them both inside.

# Chapter Eight

## The Plant Room

Unfortunately, we are not standing in Conference Room B.

I had hoped that I'd magically teleported us back to be with the rest of Year 5. Yet, when I open my eyes, I can quite clearly see:

1. This room is much, much smaller. There are no seats, no red stairs, no big screen and no stage.

2. This room has two different lights hanging down from the ceiling. One light is red, and the other is blue. The mixture of the two colours makes everything in

the room look kind of pink to purple, depending on where you look.

3. This room is full of plants. There's a shoulder-high glass box to my right with plants in it. To my left, I see a table with rows and rows of tiny plants in pots. Then straight ahead of me, is a massive window covering the entire wall and through this window I can see all different size leaves squashed up against it! It is completely and utterly covered in plants. The only gap in the window is for the black-framed door at the right of it.

4. Oh yeah, and this room has no-one else in it from Year 5 except us!

"Where are we? What is this room?" I ask Bella and Reggie.

Reggie slowly looks around the room, taking it all in before stopping in front of the plants in the glass box. He looks down at them and completely ignores me. Bella steps around him and rushes over to the glass window. She puts her hands up to the glass and then, quite suddenly, she sticks her forehead to it too.

Jumping backwards, she runs over to the black-framed door next to it. Without even a glance back at us, she opens the door wide and steps inside.

I answer my own question. "They must be growing plants," I say aloud.

Wandering around the room, I head over to the table to look at the straight rows of tiny plant cuttings all in little brown pots. These pots are all sitting in individual round brown trays and they all have neat typed labels stuck to the pots.

"P. elata," I read aloud.

"Look in here!" yells Bella, poking the top of her head out from behind the door for a moment, before hiding it again behind a large leafed plant, "It looks like an actual rainforest!"

"Really?"

"Yes!" she shouts.

As I head towards Bella's voice, I glance at Reggie. He's still standing in front of the glass box and staring at the three plants inside it. The plants have green heart-shaped leaves with dark red tips at the end.

"Come on, Reggie," I say, beckoning him to follow me as I step through the open door.

Instantly, I see exactly what Bella means. It's like an actual real-life rainforest.

There are loads of different sized plants and lots of different coloured flowers. Some plants are tall and massive with large leaves. Some are low, with small pointy leaves. There are even plants with brightly coloured flowers on long thin stems that wind around the other plants and stretch across to meet another plant that has grown taller.

The air feels hot and damp, like there is water hovering all around me, and all the leaves look fresh and slightly wet. The light in here is clear and natural, so I can see up to the glass ceiling high above me and up to the taller trees. Then, underneath my feet, is the start of a narrow stone path that looks to go through them all. The plants are all huddled in together, which means the only way to see them all is to walk along the path.

"They've created a miniature rainforest," I say to

Bella as we walk.

"Yes, to study them."

"Amazing," I reply.

Grabbing my arm, Bella points behind us. "Look at that!" A yellow stem with pink arrow shaped flowers is climbing up a thick tree trunk. She follows it with her finger. The yellow stem climbs up the tree and then moves over and continues on a different tree next to it. Up and up it goes until we can't see it anymore.

"Oh wow," I agree, before I'm distracted by a bunch of blue-green flowers hanging down on the other side of us. They look like jelly sweets all attached together and I want to reach up and pull one off. They look so tasty. I really want to eat them but even *I* know that there is *no way* that's a good idea.

Continuing on in silence, both of us take it in turns to point as we look all around. Looking down, turning around, looking up or ducking down.

Snapping me out of this strange virtual reality, Bella stops quickly and turns to face me. "Hey, we should get back or we'll miss the tour of the labs!"

"Oh no," I reply. "Boatman is going to realise we're missing. He'll ask us what we've been up to! Mr Graveshead will shout. Boatman will shout. What do we do? How do we even get back?"

"You should have just let me ask him what is going on."

"Are you kidding me? No way! You know he wouldn't have answered your question."

"He's up to no good and we need to confront him, ask him what is going on and then tell Mr Graveshead."

I pause before I reply to her. Tilting my head to the side, I look at my confusing friend. "He would have lied. There is no way that asking him would have worked out well."

"Yeah… I guess you're *probably* right. He would have lied…"

"Definitely, no doubt about it."

"What *was* he up to, though?"

As I think of a reply, the sound of running water distracts me. "What is that noise? It sounds like water splashing."

"Could it be…" Bella replies before darting off ahead of me.

It really is hot in this miniature rainforest. The sound of running water is tempting in such a heat. It sounds light and gentle, and it is coming from somewhere ahead of us.

Slightly speeding up, we take the twisting path left and under an archway of two wide plants that have grown over the path. Then, round to the left again, and we are standing in front of a waterfall.

A waterfall!

The flowing water starts incredibly high above us. It then falls through the dents and cracks of a really tall large rock before splashing into the pool underneath it. Stopping directly in front of it, the noise of the water is gentle, yet it feels strangely powerful and completely hypnotising.

Around the waterfall the plants seem thicker and wilder – There are loads of brown branches that block our way around the water to our left and to our right the many large leaves and vines have taken over the path.

"He sounded completely and utterly suspicious," continues Bella as she stares at the water flowing through the rock.

"Yeah, putting something in the kitchen and looking like it's nesting!"

"If we'd asked him why, he wouldn't have known what to say."

"I *cannot* believe you *still* think that would work, seriously? Come on. He would have asked us a question in return or just lied. Definitely, he would have completely avoided answering it and then made us feel silly or stupid… Or worse, we would have got detention! Reggie agrees with me. It's… Wait… Where is Reggie?"

"Reggie!" Bella calls out. "Reggie, you need to see this rainforest."

"He must still be in the room with the small plants."

"Why?" Bella questions, her forehead wrinkling.

"He was looking at these plants with sort of green

heart-shaped leaves with red tips on the ends. They were in a glass box. Did you see them?"

"He was?" Bella replies, her eyes opening wide and into a stare. For a moment, she just stands there staring at nothing. She looks like she has suddenly seen a vision into the future and it looks really bad.

Quickly, without saying anything, she turns back the way we came. I follow her as she marches slightly ahead of me, her brown curly hair jumping up and down behind her, and I can feel a sense of panic radiating from her. Trying to keep up, I walk back along the path again.

From this way, I can see flowers and plants that I missed the first time. It's really hard not to stop and look at the string of yellow and red flowers hanging down above my head or the orange flowers with thin leaves behind the tree.

The twisty path is back at the start before I know it. Ahead of me is the large-leaf plant covering the glass wall that I had seen when we first walked in. Then, as I turn the corner towards the door, I see Bella. She has stopped in front of the open door. Standing completely still, her hands are out in front of her as if she is about to catch a ball. Puzzled, I step towards her and look through the doorway in the direction of her fixed stare.

It's Reggie.

He's crouched down in front of the glass box, his hands pressed against the glass. His eyes are open wide and he has a smile on his face that stretches sideways rather than going up. It is a strange, intense smile. I saw him do the exact same smile last month when we walked past the toyshop in town. They had a massive LEGO set in the window and Reggie said it was the all-time best ever LEGO set that he really wanted for his birthday.

"I know this plant," he says without looking at us, as we step past the open door and into the room. "It's on their website. This is the plant. THIS IS IT."

"This is what?" I ask.

"Reggie, what are you up to?" Bella says slowly. As I watch Reggie and try to work out what is going on, I can hear the sound of Bella closing the door behind us. "We need to get back," says Bella, really slowly, sounding out each word clearly as if Reggie might not be able to understand her. "We need to get back to Conference Room—"

"I'm only going to be a sec."

"NO!" Bella screams from behind me, the sudden loud noise knocking me off balance. Shocked by her scream, I turn to face her. She's leaping forward, her arms out in front of her, diving towards Reggie. In that second, I realise this must be bad. Quickly, I turn back towards Reggie, ready to push him away from the glass box and away from whatever Bella is screaming about.

But we're too late.

Reggie's hands were already on the two glass doors in front of him. He has already undone the small plastic clasp holding the doors shut and, with us diving towards him, he lifts the plant up.

"Wait!" he shouts back as us, standing up while holding his precious plant in both hands. "No sudden movements!" he shouts again, the strange smile on his face replaced with a look of fear.

I can hear him, but I'm already leaping towards him. Bella can hear him, but she's already diving through the air.

A quick turn mid-air.

A quick stop mid-leap.

A crash of shoulders and arms.

A fall to the side.

A step back from Reggie.

A fall to the floor from Bella and me.

A near miss.

So close.

Until I knock Reggie's foot.

All it took was a shake to the base of the plant pot and the leaves quivered. A quiver that picks up speed. A quiver that keeps going long after the pot has stopped moving. A quiver that seems to be blurring my view of the red tips on the heart-shaped leaves.

Slowly at first, a gas appears near the red tips of the leaves and forms into a cloud around the plant.

Then, the cloud quickly spreads.

With Reggie still holding the pot up, the cloud bursts down to the floor, spreading down and out to the sides. The cloud races towards Bella and me as we remain on the floor, covering us before hitting the glass wall behind. Travelling up all the walls, it fills the space with the cloud as it reaches up to the ceiling. The air smells sweet, yet it is wet. There are large droplets of liquid all over me, which prickle my skin. I can't brush them off. I close my eyes as my skin feels tight and stretched. Then, when I open them again, I can see nothing: Absolutely and completely nothing in the room at all.

# Chapter Nine

## Vanished

Everything has disappeared. Everything that made me call this room The Plant Room, has vanished.

The table and the small plant cuttings have vanished. The glass box with the heart-shaped leaf plants inside it has vanished. Reggie, the plant he's holding, and Bella by my side, have also all vanished. The lights on the ceiling have vanished and now the only light coming through to this room is the light through the glass from the next-door rainforest.

Oh yes, and the other thing that's very strange is that I HAVE VANISHED TOO.

"Aghhhhh!" I scream out to the empty room.

If I have vanished and I can't see my hands or legs, then am I really here? Yes. I'm here because my thoughts are here and my voice is here. Plus, I can feel my toes when I curl them, I can feel my hands if I think about clenching my fists, and I can touch my nose if I really concentrate.

*Ow, that was my eye.*

I JUST CANNOT SEE MY HAND… Or my legs. Or my arms.

I scream again. "This is hurting my head!"

"This cannot be happening!" Bella's voice shouts next to me.

"Bella!" I shout back.

"What have you two done?" screams a high-pitched Reggie-sounding voice.

"Reggie? You're both here! Can you see me? I can't see you. Where is everything? Have my eyes had a cosmic film put over them so I can see through people? Can I now see through people… and things?"

"Clara," Bella's low voice breaks in. "Everything in the room has turned invisible."

"What?!"

"It's the plant's defence mechanism! I was trying to warn you!" says the high-pitched Reggie-sounding voice.

"A defence mechanism," I mumble.

"Don't you start with us!" Bella's voice booms out next to me. Her voice has moved so that it sounds like she is now standing up and in front of Reggie. "I know all about its defence mechanism – I was trying to warn *you*! If you knew, then why did you open the box!?"

"I was just going to look at it," answers Reggie.

"What, you can't look through transparent glass!?"

"You both knew?" I ask, cutting in to their argument. "You both knew that this plant has a defence mechanism that does this? What is this? How can a plant do this?"

If I could see their faces right now, I know they would both be looking at me like a giant massive sigh

– It's kind of like an eye roll mixed in with a deep breath before you explain the obvious to someone.

"Clara, didn't you look at the BioZone website at all this weekend?" asks Bella.

"No, I didn't! I was too busy researching Merihal."

"Oh OK, well, this plant was a massive discovery. A team were in the depths of The Valdivian Rainforest researching another set of plants when they found it. Basically, when it thinks it's about to be attacked, it releases a gas that's stored in the tips of its leaves. The gas is so powerful that it turns itself and everything nearby invisible. There's a whole new team researching it and—"

"And Reggie set it off," I whisper.

"No, *you* set it off!" he shouts. "I can still hear you, you know!"

"You opened the box," says Bella with a stern voice.

"She hit my foot!"

"But you picked it up!" she replies. "Who does that?"

"It's done!" I scream over them both in a really

weird screechy way that doesn't quite sound like my voice, even though it definitely came from me. "It's done!" I shout again to see if my voice is any less weird. No, it's still sounding very high and screechy. "And now we need to work out how to get back to our group, continue the tour, turn ourselves back from being completely and utterly invisible without Mr Graveshead knowing or Boatman – especially Boatman – I feel he would be completely and utterly worse than Mr Graveshead and I can't believe that I'm saying that or that there is someone worse than Mr Graveshead – so, neither of them must know, no-one must know, and Those Two must never know, AND we need to work out what Boatman is up to…"

I can't stop talking – The words just seem to keep coming out. I'm doing Bella's 'speaking in one long sentence with no space for breaths' thing. This is usually what Bella does when she panics. It feels like the right thing to do right now, and it is kind of making me feel a lot better.

"Clara," says Bella, jumping in when I finally decide

to breathe. "You're right."

"I am?"

"Boatman is up to something and we need to find out what it is."

"Oh, I'm not sure I was—"

"And, you're right that he would lie to us if we asked him about any of it."

"Oh, right, yes, he would," I mutter. My head is spinning a bit. My eyes are going a bit weird too. I think it's the empty room, the voices and knowing that I am here sitting on the floor, yet I cannot *see* myself sitting on the floor.

"So," Bella says slowly. "We need to get his phone so we have proof, and then he can't lie to us."

"Huh?"

"The proof will be on his phone. We grab that and then we ask him what is going on."

"Ask him?"

"We'll have proof, he won't be able to lie to us."

"But we're invisible," I remind her.

"Which is perfect – we can get his phone without

him knowing!" she exclaims.

My head is so dizzy now. I need to close my eyes. Even though I can't see Bella and Reggie, or see my own body, closing my eyes helps. It stops the spinning.

"Look, Bella, we're invisible," I say slowly. "So even if we had his phone, we couldn't do anything with it. We need to change back."

"Grab his phone first though, right?"

"No, we need to change back!"

"No, we need to find out what he's up to!"

"We need to change back and then we can… Wait, hold on," I say, stopping the argument between us as memories of me running around the school on my own and being mistaken for a mouse come flooding back to me. "Whatever we do, we need to stay together."

"Yes, definitely stay together!" agrees Bella with a small laugh.

"Hey," Reggie cuts in, his voice sounding normal again, "Mrs Elliot is here at BioZone today."

"She is!" I shout with delight.

"She's with Year 6," continues Reggie. "She would be a great teacher to find. We could tell her what's going on."

"She would be SO MUCH better than Mr Graveshead or asking Boatman any questions at all whatsoever. Ever," I say, agreeing with Reggie. "Don't you think, Bella?"

There is a pause as Bella doesn't reply. I know she desperately wants to ask Mr Netship what he's up to, but going to Mrs Elliot has got to be a better option. I open my eyes, realise it's no use as I still feel dizzy and then close them again.

"OK," begins Bella. "We get his phone and then we go to Mrs Elliot."

"Yes," I say, feeling like this is a good plan. I can breathe a bit better now. Mrs Elliot will ask all the questions and my 'Rule Number Two: No Questions' can remain safe. No tricks. No questions answered with questions. No shouting and not listening. Breathe. Breathe.

"We must make sure we stay together, though. It's

going to be so easy to lose each other," warns Reggie.

"Reggie," says Bella in a similar low warning tone, "are you still holding onto the plant that just turned us invisible?"

# Chapter Ten

## Not Really That Easy

'm standing in the white corridor again. I look up at the row of spotlights and then down at the grey floor below. I hear the door to The Plant Room closing behind me and I continue to stare out at the long, empty corridor.

"I think—"

"Aghhhhh, Reggie!" I yell at his voice, jumping backwards and knocking into the wall. "I thought you were over by the door!"

"Clara! Sorry, I was wondering where you were."

"I'm here," says Bella to my right.

Reggie coughs. "I was just saying, I think when we ran away from Boatman, we went right when we should have gone left… Shall I go first?" he adds.

Getting out of the invisible room with my invisible friends and not being able to see the invisible door handle, was hard work. Yet now, our plan is to get all the way back to Conference Room B.

"How am I going to know?!" I question, looking up and down at the empty corridor. "How am I going to know if you've gone first or even where you are? We are going to completely and utterly lose each other."

"We'll link arms," suggests Bella, her voice suddenly really close.

I sigh. "Bella, that's my head."

"Oops, sorry."

"Hey, I know, I'll sing!" exclaims Reggie. "Then you'll know where I am."

This is *not* going to be easy.

*This* is going to be hard work.

*＊＊＊*

Humming his way along the corridor, Reggie is actually quite tuneful. My brain is still going completely crazy, though; I can *feel* Bella's arm linking through mine; I can *hear* Reggie humming ahead of me. Yet, the only thing I can *see* is the grey floor and empty white corridor all around me.

*CLICK! CLUNK!*

A loud noise comes from somewhere ahead of us.

With it echoing around the walls, Reggie stops humming. He stops moving too and so does Bella, so I walk into both of them.

"Owww!"

"Shush!"

"My foot!"

"Wait, shush."

"What is it?" I ask.

As if answering my question, a man slightly taller than me, in a dark grey suit and pink tie appears ahead of us. Turning towards us, he strides down the corridor.

The problem is, this man's walk is very *unusual* –
His arms are swinging around absolutely everywhere,
like they're punching the air all around him! He's
taking up the whole corridor with his strange air-
punching walk and he's heading straight for where we
are standing.

This is bad. Really bad.

All three of us instinctively get closer and closer to
the wall.

It's no use. I am invisible, but I'm still actually
standing here. He's going to stride down the corridor
straight into us. His swinging arms and air-punching
walk is going to knock the three of us over.

I wish I could walk through walls.

OK, I can do this. I'm ready. I'll duck and dive. If I
watch the punches, I can try to duck and avoid a clash
with my nose and then I'll dive behind him. I've done
super stunt-like superhero moves like this before. I
can do it again.

As I stretch, bend my knees and get ready to spring

into action, the man in the dark grey suit stops. He's about a metre in front of us as we huddle by the wall. Can he hear us? I mustn't breathe. Can he see us? Can he read minds? Does he know we are standing right in front of him?

With a brief look over his shoulder, the man turns back to face us again. Quickly, his hand flies up to his face. Then, in one swift move, his thumb goes right into his nose.

*Ewwwwwwwwwwww!* He has stopped walking down the corridor so he can pick his nose. Adults don't pick their noses!

Dad is always telling me not to pick my nose. Sometimes, I forget. I forget and then I forget that I'm also not allowed to eat it. I honestly forget that I'm not allowed to. I do quite like how salty it tastes, though.

As I stare at this man picking his nose and wonder if he will eat it, I can feel Bella gently tugging and pulling my arm. Reggie and Bella must have crept past this air-punching walker while he's standing completely still with his thumb in his nose – and before he starts up again.

Quickly, I do the same. Shuffling along next to the wall, I keep watching him in case he moves. I'm close. I hold my breath, and as I squeeze past him, he brings his thumb out, looks at it and then puts a finger in his nose instead.

*Ewwwwwwwwwww!*

I continue to slide past the 'air-punching walker who picks his nose' and get ready to take a big step. I'm ready to duck and then dive right behind him in one quick and stealth-like motion. I am so close to being completely past him and utterly free from danger.

Placing my left foot down, the ground underneath it moves. It wobbles. It slides. Something's wrong.

I think I've trodden on Bella!

Stumbling on the missed step, I spin a little too fast, trying not to fall over but forgetting about my right foot.

"Hey, what was that?" says the man as I kick him in the knee.

Oops.

Abandoning his nose picking, he bends down to rub his knee as I quickly stumble backwards to move my right foot out the way.

"That was weird," he says to the empty corridor. "Strange," he adds as he stops rubbing his knee.

I take a quiet breath and reach out to touch the wall next to me. The 'air-punching walker who picks his nose' stands up straight, slowly walks a few steps away from us, stops, rubs his knee again and then carries on walking.

As I watch him stride off down the corridor again, I let out my held breath. I only realise that I'm walking slowly backwards when I bump into Bella. "That was *so* close!" I whisper.

"I thought he was going to walk right into me," replies Reggie, standing right next to me and making me jump again.

"Ewwww, he picked his nose," Bella whispers.

"Hey, that need for a nose-pick just saved us," laughs Reggie.

Back in formation with Reggie humming and leading the way, we continue down the long corridor. I'm finding the humming quite peaceful, really. It's like it's stopping me from feeling so completely scared that we are invisible and are on a mission to find Mr Netship and get his phone.

Breathe.

Listen to the humming.

Breathe.

With a right turn from Bella ahead of me, I can see Conference Room B at the end of the corridor.

"So," whispers Reggie. "We'll go in, find Boatman, grab his phone and then come straight back out and look for Mrs Elliot and Year 6."

This is our Plan A.

The finer details took a lot of negotiating with Bella but luckily Reggie agreed with me – It would be a bad idea to ask Mr Netship anything and best left for Mrs Elliot. I'm not entirely happy with the 'grab his phone' part of Plan A but very happy with the 'look for Mrs Elliot' part. If anyone can help us with this turning invisible problem, surely it's our school science teacher. The good thing about this plan is that Reggie has volunteered to actually *grab* the phone, and really, all I need to do is stay with them and not get lost.

"Let's creep in," says Bella, and I can feel a tug from her hand as she moves towards the slightly open door.

As soon as we step through and into Conference Room B, I hear a woman's voice speaking. It's coming out of the speakers all around the room. There looks like there might be something happening on the stage.

"Scientists must constantly question their findings," she says as I tiptoe round from the door and towards the stage so I can see her. She has a head microphone on that goes over the top of her head and round to her mouth, square glasses on her nose and blonde hair tied back. "How can we learn anything if we don't," she continues, as I bump into the back of Bella who has weirdly stopped moving.

"Oh no!" Bella whispers, sending a sense of panic straight through my whole body. Quickly turning away from facing the stage, I see why she's stopped.

This is not our group. This is not Year 5.

Sitting on the rows of seats that we had been sitting on earlier, are the whole of Year 6. And there at the front, with a pen and notebook in her hands, is Mrs Elliot.

# Chapter Eleven

## The Wrong Place

rs Elliot is right in front of me! My cure for this terrible problem, which really was not my fault... Well, OK, *this time* it was a little bit my fault. The point is, though, she is right there. She can help us with this disastrous situation we have found ourselves in... again... and we don't need to grab Mr Netship's phone first because we can tell Mrs Elliot and she can help.

All I need to do is walk over to her.

"So, with this in mind," says the woman on the

stage behind me into her microphone, her voice coming out of the speakers all around the room. "I'm going to open it up to the floor."

The thing is, I can't really just tap Mrs Elliot on the arm. I am invisible. An invisible tap on the arm is certainly going to make her jump or scream. I could whisper in her ear, but she might think there's a ghost next to her. Either way, everyone will turn to look while she loudly tries to work out who is saying her name or why it feels like someone's tapping her on the shoulder. A really bad idea.

"You've heard me talking for a while now," continues the woman on the stage. "So, do you have any questions you'd like to ask?"

Wait, what did I just hear? Did the woman on the stage behind me just say *any questions*?

No. No-one's going to ask her a question. It's a classic teacher trick that this teacher-like person on stage is using! She just said to everyone that she's been talking for ages – She wants to know if they've all been listening. Everyone knows it. Year 6 will DEFINITELY know it's a trick.

Turning around to face the woman on stage, my Rule Number Two: No Questions alarm automatically starts flashing in my head.

But then it stumbles.

The woman is standing at the edge of the stage and she's smiling. With this, her eyes are slowly moving across all the Year 6 faces in front of her. She's not moving away and trying to get off the stage. She also doesn't look like she would shout if someone did want to ask a question. She looks like she might *actually* want to answer a question. I stare in disbelief at this smiling woman with her hands clasped together in front of her. She looks... well ... eager.

Spinning back round, my Rule Number Two: No Questions alarm has completely paused. It's unsure what to do. Looking quickly across the rows of seats, I can see there are loads of hands up in the air. Right up in the air. There must be, like, eighteen of them.

Is this some kind of special and magical place where it's OK to ask a question, and you won't feel silly or get a question in return? Surely, they must all be thinking that it would be easier to look up the answer on the internet at home. You know, just in case they do ask a question that has already been answered.

"I'll help!" shouts Mrs Elliot as she jumps up from her seat. She points at Isla in the furthest corner of the room.

"What's the weirdest thing you or your team have found?" shouts Isla.

Quickly, I turn back to the woman on the stage. "Oh, good question," she replies, and I stare at her, not blinking at all. "There are many plants still being discovered, and these new plants have properties we don't know about. Unfortunately, for us all, places like the Amazonian rainforest are still being destroyed at an alarming rate and this kills things we don't even know about yet. But, to answer your question," she says slowly, pausing and looking up at the corner of the room. "Yes," she continues, turning back to look at Isla. "For me, it still has to be the vanishing red. Found on the forest floor under the dense canopy in

The Valdivian Rainforest, this plant looks like any normal plant you might come across. It has green heart-shaped leaves with dark red tips at the end of them. Except, the vanishing red has a defence mechanism that turns itself and everything around it invisible if it thinks it's being attacked! You may have heard about it. Have you all seen it on our website?"

Spinning back around again, I can see nearly every single person in the room nod their head… except me. Fine! I know I should have definitely looked this place up on the internet before we came here. Yes, perhaps if I had, then I wouldn't have left Reggie alone staring at a plant that can turn us invisible.

The thing is though, she's answering Isla's question. No tricks. No getting her to repeat everything she remembers so that she can answer her own question. She's just answering it.

"It's amazing to think that such a plant exists," she continues. "The team have worked out that certain UV rays from the sun fade the invisibility—"

"It fades," I whisper.

"This, of course, could take some time in a rainforest under such a dense canopy. It is thought that in that time the attacker would become disorientated and move away from the plant. There is still so much to learn from this plant, and we have a great team researching it."

"Oooooo, I wish I could ask her a question," whispers Bella close to my ear.

"Me too," I reply. I'm surprised with my reply, but I do. I want to ask her:

1. How does it fade?
2. Does it always fade?
3. Does it fade evenly, or might my head come back first so it looks like it's floating in mid-air? Or maybe a leg and an arm and then an hour later my other arm?
4. Could it last forever?
5. Are there any side-effects?
6. Should I be able to walk through walls?

"We are also questioning," says the woman on stage, "whether certain species of animal use this plant as a protection against predators. Perhaps to hide under or lay their eggs."

I have so many questions in my head right now but I don't think the internet will have any of the answers. Usually, I look EVERYTHING up on the internet but right now the expert is this woman right here on the stage in front of me.

"This is all great, but it's not what I want to ask," I whisper.

"Really?!" replies Bella a bit too loudly. "*You* want to ask *her* a question."

"Shush, but yes, I do."

"What about your *rule*?"

"Huh?"

"Your rule... You said you wanted to ask a question."

Bella's right. I feel so confused.

Bella may think my No Questions rule is silly, but it protects me. It stops me making a mistake and falling for tricks. It stops eye rolls and tuts and sighs and anyone laughing at me. It stops me feeling stupid and embarrassed. It stops me having to stand up in front of the whole class and try to work out the answer to the question I just asked. I don't want to make that mistake again. But... right now, this woman is probably the only person who can answer them. What do I do, stay invisible forever because I don't ask questions?

"Well, erm, I don't know," I whisper back to Bella.

"Clara," she says, laughing and hugging my arm. "We'll be OK. We will stick to the plan and we'll be OK."

"The problem is, we shouldn't even be here. Where is Year 5? Where is Boatman?"

Maybe we need a Plan B.

# chapter Twelve

## Plan B

Telepathy is still not working.

I've tried asking about ten questions to the woman on the stage through telepathy and she has not answered any of them.

"Our ocean plants do absorb carbon dioxide, just like plants on land," she says, answering Penelope's question. "Unfortunately, the sea itself is absorbing too much carbon dioxide, and this is warming up the sea, which is not good for aquatic life."

I've also tried telepathy with Mrs Elliot and she

doesn't look like she has any idea I'm here. The thing is:

1. The woman on stage is not answering any of my questions.
2. We have no idea where Mr Netship and Year 5 are.
3. Mrs Elliot is still there, right in front of me.

So, I'm moving to Plan B.

I thought of it as soon as I saw Mrs Elliot, and now I definitely think it is the right thing to do: I'm going to walk over to her while everyone else is distracted with questions and tell her what's happened. She can help us with this invisibility thing and she will definitely know how to find out what Mr Netship is up to. The cure to all of our problems is standing there pushing her round brown glasses back on her nose as she listens to how our oceans need to be protected. I'll whisper, '*Mrs Elliot, it's Clara*' and she will immediately know what has happened and she won't scream. Mainly because she doesn't really seem like the 'scared of ghosts' type of person, but also because she just heard about this exact 'invisible defence' thing.

Deciding that it's now or never, I let go of my tight grip on Bella's arm and I step forward.

"What are you doing?" hisses Bella as she finds my right arm and pulls me back again. "We mustn't lose each other."

"Mrs Elliot is right there."

"So?"

"She can help us."

"No, stick to the plan."

"Trust me, I have a Plan B and it's perfect."

"No," Bella says again as I boldly walk towards Mrs Elliot. Since Bella still has hold of my arm, I end up pulling her forwards with me.

"She can help," I explain, as Bella keeps hold of my arm. "She can sort this whole mess out."

Pulling Bella forwards again, she then pulls me back. I pull her forwards and she pulls me back.

"Bella, let go of my arm."

Completely caught up in this tug-of-war argument

(where I'm trying to quietly argue with an invisible Bella and I'm not 100% sure I'm actually looking at her), neither of us have noticed George from Year 6. He is sneaking back into the room through the open door we used.

"No, Clara, don't do it," Bella says.

Pausing from dragging Bella along by my arm, I turn back to face where I think Bella is standing. "Why?" I question.

"We need to get the phone first! It's the only way. Come on, we should go... Wait, watch out!"

"What?"

*BASH!*

A painful whack on my back. "Owwwwww."

A moment of falling before colliding with Bella.

*THUD!*

"Aghhhhh."

*THUMP!*

A very painful bump as I land on the floor.

"Owwwwww," Bella, George and I all say together.

"George?!" says Mrs Godden, the Year 6 class

teacher, jumping up from her seat at the top of the red stairs.

"George, are you OK?" Mrs Elliot asks, stepping forward.

"I...I...I... What happened?"

Making a confident sprint to his seat, George has run straight into an invisible force-field (me), has knocked his nose mid-air (on the back on my head), and has been thrown backwards (while I have been thrown forward and have collided with Bella).

"Are you OK?" the woman on stage asks him.

"I'm sorry," he replies, looking up at her.

*Owwwww!* My back hurts from George running into it, my right arm really hurts from landing on it and I think I twisted my left wrist. As I continue lying on the floor, I can feel the black scratchy carpet underneath me as I hold my painful wrist in towards me.

But it's just not safe. I need to move.

I can see Mrs Godden running down the stairs towards George and towards me. If I stay here, she'll run straight into me and I'll send her flying through the air with her arms out in front of her like Superman. Then, what if more people run down the stairs? They will all end up lying on the floor after tripping over the same strange invisible force-field.

I need to get out of the way and quickly.

Finding the energy to move, I log roll towards the stage.

"Clara?" Bella whispers as I keep rolling and rolling towards the stage.

"I'm here," I reply once I've stopped rolling. Looking in the direction her voice came from, it sounds like she is somewhere next to me and by the stage.

"Make your way towards the entrance door," she replies. "Reggie's already there."

Looking over towards the door we came in through when we first entered Conference Room B at the beginning of the day, I can see it slowly and magically opening.

"Did you trip over?" I hear Mrs Godden ask

George, as I shuffle towards Reggie.

"I... But why does my nose hurt? It feels like I walked into something."

"You were running," Mrs Godden replies sternly. "You must have hit your nose on the floor."

"Oh right," he replies, sounding unconvinced.

Reaching the end of the stage, I get up and walk towards the open door.

"Reggie?" Bella whispers. Hearing her voice, I reach out and find her arm. I really don't want to lose her. "Reggie, where are you?" she asks.

"I'm here."

Walking towards his voice, I reach out, ready to hold his arm too. My arm feels shaky. My whole body feels shaky. I'm not sure I can deal with being invisible anymore, let alone not being able to see my friends.

"I was so close to reaching Mrs Elliot," I whisper to them both. "She could have helped us. You know Mrs Elliot would be great at this sort of thing."

"Clara, don't you see?" Reggie replies. "We don't want to be turned back yet. We're invisible. We have a superpower."

"A superpower?"

"Plus, we know it fades, because she said so," whispers Bella. "So really the question is, how much time do we have?"

Linking arms altogether, I let Reggie and Bella walk through the open door first as I turn to see how George is getting on. In the middle of Mrs Godden clapping her hands together to settle Year 6, is a confused George walking slowly back to his seat. Then I spot Mrs Elliot. She is standing where George fell over and is staring straight at us as if she can completely see us.

"We have a superpower," I repeat in a whisper before following Reggie and Bella through the open door.

# Chapter Thirteen

## What Superheroes Do

Reggie is, of course, right... WE HAVE A SUPERPOWER! So awesome.

OK, so I can't read minds or talk through telepathy. I'm not going to give up on trying, though. And we can't walk through walls. Walking through walls would save so much time. Still, we have the power of INVISIBILITY!

The incident with George has given us a great idea.

"You trip Boatman up. I'll grab his phone," says Reggie.

"He'll be so confused, he won't know what's happening," concludes Bella.

Back to Plan A, only better: We are going to make it look like Mr Netship fell over by accident and just happened to lose his phone. There won't be any questions, it can all be done quickly and without any shouting or anything. Plus, we now know where Mrs Elliot is, so we can run straight back to her.

"We'd better hurry though," I add.

Standing outside Conference Room B, we are in the entrance hall. It is a big semi-circular room with a bright blue carpet. To the left of the semi-circle are two doors for the toilets' and to my right is another door that I have no idea where it goes. Ahead of where I'm standing is a giant wall of windows and glass doors. If we went through one of the glass doors, it would take us out to the grey path with neat green bushes either side and back to the coaches.

"Look, there's a site map!" whispers Bella.

I don't know where she's pointing or where she's gone, so I look around the walls. There are loads of

giant posters showing people, plants and places and…
Oh yeah, a 'You Are Here' map. Mum and Dad love
standing in front of 'You Are Here' maps whenever we
go anywhere. I just want to move and start looking at
stuff, BUT we have to wait while they study the map.
Boring. Darren doesn't care, he's always bored anyway
and besides, he just stands there listening to music
through his big red headphones. However, today, a
'You Are Here' map is *actually* the best thing ever.

"There's Conference Room B," I say, pointing to the
map even though they can't see my hand.

"Our group is meant to be touring the labs…" says
Bella.

I scan my eyes over the map. There are a lot of
laboratory rooms. There is actually an entire *zone* of
them coloured in light blue.

"Looks like the best way is through that mysterious
door next to us," I say, looking at the map and then
over at the door. According to the map, the door leads
us to a corridor. This goes past a kitchen and a
cleaning cupboard, and onwards to another door at

the edge of the large light blue LABORATORY ZONE.

"Yes, looks better than trying to go outside, round the building that way and to the main entrance there," agrees Reggie.

"Yep," says Bella, and I can feel her hand grab my arm.

As soon as we walk across the bright blue carpet, step through the doorway and into the corridor, a warm sweet sugary smell enters my nose. It's a delicious baking smell that makes my mouth salivate and my tummy rumble.

"Hey," I whisper to my invisible friends in the dark quiet corridor as we creep along it. "I know we have this superpower and we are on like a superhero mission or whatever, but… I'm hungry."

"Hungry?!" asks Bella.

Stopping suddenly in the doorway to the kitchen, I can see the source of that incredible smell. "We didn't get a snack at snack time."

"This is no time to stop for snacks."

"But look," I say, pulling Bella's hand so she doesn't

carry on walking. I'm hoping that she can see what I can see. "There's the snack trolley from earlier."

Ahead of us and in the kitchen is the metal snack trolley. It's next to the wall with the remains of the delicious snacks on top. I can even see a plate on a metal stand with five cinnamon buns waiting to be eaten.

"That's called stealing!" hisses Bella.

"No, it's not. It's called, 'We didn't get to have a snack earlier, so, technically, they are ours and we are just eating them a little later than we should have.'"

"Hey," cuts in Reggie, "I'm actually quite hungry too. It would be good to fuel up before we take on Boatman. And Clara's right, we won't take more than what they would have let us have earlier... you know?"

Bella sighs. "Oh, fine!"

"Yes!" I can almost taste it now. "Are we all going for the cinnamon buns?"

"Shush, I can hear someone in there," whispers Bella.

She's right. Over the loud sounds of my tummy

rumbling, I can hear noises. It sounds like a heavy metal door opening and closing and plates knocking together.

"If there are people in there, then we can't just float three cinnamon buns out of the room and expect them not to find that strange," continues Bella.

"We'll take one each and sneak them out," I reply. "It'll be fine. Come on Bella. I'm so hungry."

Leading the way, I creep into the kitchen with Bella and Reggie behind me. The weird thing about being invisible is that it takes a bit of getting used to that people can't actually see you. Even though I can't see Bella or Reggie, I pause as I spot the man and the woman behind the door and over the other side of the room. A sudden stop that sends Bella walking straight into me.

"You finished?" asks the woman as she opens the oven door, takes out a baking tray full of giant pastries and places it on a metal rack beside her.

"Yeah, nearly done," says the man, stacking the cups and plates onto a white plastic tray next to him.

They are both wearing white aprons over their black T-shirts and black trousers. I recognise the woman from earlier. She was the one who came into Conference Room B with the snack trolley.

"I'll put the kettle on then, and we'll have a break before the next group."

Having convinced myself that they can't see us, I continue to sneak over to the snack trolley. The cinnamon buns look amazing. They're big, with extra cinnamon and brown sugar sprinkled on top. Squeezing behind the trolley, my eyes scan the plate. Before I can grab it though, the biggest bun flies high up into the air, does a double flip and lands in the bananas.

"Reggie!" Bella scolds.

"What did you say?" says the woman in front of us as the kettle clicks off.

"Me?" says the man.

"You say something?"

"No, nothing."

Holding my breath, I freeze on the spot and stare at

the two adults in front of us. Reggie's cinnamon bun is sitting on the bananas, completely unmoving.

"Oh, I thought I heard something," continues the woman. "Perhaps it was a kid's voice, maybe…"

"So many children here today. So loud! It's like *bring your kid to work day*."

"I know! Not right all these kids here with all this technology and what not. Something's going to go wrong. I tell you; I can feel it in my bones."

With their backs still to us, the two adults carry on with what they're doing. My heart is beating so hard. I'm so nervous. Hungry but nervous.

Choosing carefully and choosing quickly, I take the next biggest bun off the plate and hide it behind the row of crisp packets underneath. Immediately, another cinnamon bun jumps off the plate and lands next to mine. I look up at the man and the woman; they both still have their backs to us.

"OK, let's go," I whisper.

After a slight pause, the bun sitting on the bananas jumps to life. It bobs up and down, bouncing over the apples and across the trolley towards the door.

"Oh goodness me," whispers Bella with a sigh. Slower and with less bouncing, Bella slides her cinnamon bun across the trolley.

I look down at my cinnamon bun in my invisible hand and then up at the adults. Taking a deep breath and with a trembling hand, I move the bun from behind the crisp packets and follow Bella. At the edge of the trolley, my shaking cinnamon bun jumps down to about 10cm from the floor. It's like controlling a puppet and bringing it to life on a stage for a whole audience to see. Except, my plan is that they won't look down here and if they do, then I can quickly drop it.

Floating the bun 10cm above the ground, I shuffle quickly towards the door. I'm watching the two adults as I do this, checking to see if either of them turns around. As the woman pours the milk into the mugs and the man reaches up to the top cupboard, three cinnamon buns delicately float 10cm off the ground behind them and out the door.

# Chapter Fourteen

## A Knock

That cinnamon bun was probably the best cinnamon bun I have ever tasted. I ate it slowly as we walked down the corridor. It was delicious. And now, as we stand at the edge of the LABORATORY ZONE, I finish the last few little bits of sugar and cinnamon floating in front of me on my invisible hands.

The LABORATORY ZONE.

This is what the map called the large section of laboratory rooms coloured in light blue. I thought with a name like that, it would be really dark but there would be loads of small different coloured lights flashing all around us. There would be tiny green lights on the floor too, guiding the way, and a small door to go through. Perhaps there would be smoke coming from under the door and a great big SHHH noise coming from somewhere unknown. This is all pretty much what I imagine entering an alien space ship to be like.

No. It's nothing like that at all. It is just a black door at the end of a corridor with a big window in it.

"We need a key pass," whispers Reggie.

"A what?" I reply.

"The door is locked, but there is this box here that looks like you put your key pass up against it to open the door."

"We could see if there is a spare key pass in the kitchen," suggests Bella. "Maybe one of them has put their pass down on the side. We could quickly borrow it, open the door and then put it back while one of us keeps the door open."

"Yes, good plan, or there might be one in that cleaning cupboard next to us," adds Reggie. "You know, they might keep a spare one in there."

"Oh yeah, that's a good idea," agrees Bella.

"Or we could just knock on the door?" I add.

Immediately, Bella and Reggie go completely quiet. Their silence keeps on going and I'm kind of glad I can't see their faces.

"I've seen it in a film," I continue. "There's a security guard sitting right there, look." I drum lightly on the window, trying to show them the man with the white shirt and a badge that says 'SECURITY' on it. He's sitting at a table, tapping away on a keyboard as he looks at the computer screen in front of him. "We knock at the door and the security guard will open it because he's confused and can't work out where the knocking is coming from."

As my words linger in the air and are met with more silence, I wonder if Bella and Reggie are still standing there. It feels like I'm completely and utterly talking to myself.

"There is *no way* that is going to work," Reggie finally says.

"Yeaaaaaaaah that is completely not going to work," agrees Bella.

Before I change my mind, and also because I'm slightly annoyed with them both, I loudly knock on the door. I can see the man through the window look straight at me and then turn back to his computer screen. He doesn't move from his seat.

"Seeeeee!" gloats Reggie.

"Well, it never works the first time!" I reply and immediately knock again harder, taking my annoyance out on the door. On the second knock, the security guard pushes his chair away from the table, gets up and moves towards the door. As he gets closer to the door, it makes a noise.

*BEEEEEEEEP*

"Hello?" says the security guard, sticking his head out of the doorway.

It's very hard not to automatically say 'hello' back to him, especially as we are standing right in front of him. He's about 40cm away from me and is strangely looking right at me. The problem is, he is also standing completely and utterly in our way. This is NOT how it goes in all the films I've watched.

Thinking fast, because I want this plan to work so I can say 'I told you so' to Reggie, I move and knock on the door to the cleaning cupboard. He looks at where I just knocked and darts towards it.

"Hello?" he questions again.

Jumping out of the way, I just miss him crashing into me as I squash myself against the wall. I guess that Reggie and Bella have already managed to get past him. Side-stepping next to the wall, I head towards the door to the LABORATORY ZONE.

"Hello?" he says again as he opens the door to the cleaning cupboard. "Anyone there? Everything OK? Why can I hear knocking?!"

While the security guard talks to an empty cleaning cupboard, I seize the opportunity to leap through the open door. As I leap, I bump straight into Reggie, who I think bumps into Bella. We rush to get through the door, stumbling over each other as the man comes back. As I trip over Reggie's leg, I can hear him trying not to giggle. I'm trying not to laugh too, as I finally free my foot, twist round and fall backwards.

Watching the security guard follow us and close the door behind him, he spreads his hand across his forehead. "That was weird," he mutters, moving back to the table where he was sitting before. "I think I need more sleep... Yes, more sleep or maybe less coffee."

***

The corridors in the LABORATORY ZONE are different from the white corridors we got lost in before. They do still have the same grey floor, but the white walls have been replaced with big glass windows. This means that while we walk down the corridor, we can see into each and every room.

A few of the rooms we pass are small, with only two rows of white tables either side, while the other rooms are much bigger. These bigger rooms have long white tables in the centre of them and different machines around the sides.

"Look," says Bella, nudging me. Taking my hand, she lifts it up and points it towards a window on my left. Immediately, I see a person completely covered in blue plastic! They look like they're wearing a bright blue plastic onesie made out of carrier bags. It goes right over their head and all the way down to the bottom of their shoes. Along with this blue plastic onesie, they have on clear plastic goggles and thick dark blue rubber gloves. Standing close to the window, they are next to a white table with a huge grey metal box on top of it. Opening the glass hatch on the grey box, they slowly and carefully place a very small dish inside it.

"I wonder what's in that dish," whispers Bella.

I'm not sure either. "Looks like red jelly or something."

Closing the hatch slowly, the person then presses the buttons on the side of the grey box. Three green lights come on one at a time, then the person in the onesie cautiously takes four steps back.

"Whaaaaat?" I breathe. I'm wondering and waiting – my mind is wondering if it is safe to stand here and also waiting to see what's going to happen to the jelly. Might the whole thing explode?

"This place is am-a-zing," sings Reggie quietly from the other side of Bella.

With the person in the blue onesie walking to the other side of the lab, I feel Bella gently tugging my arm. "Look," she whispers, pulling me along. "Look in here," she adds, stopping in front of the next window.

This next room is completely full of different plants: There are plants covering the tables around the side of the room, plants grouped together under sections of white lights, and there are a few plants next to the microscopes on the middle table.

I scan them all quickly. "I can't see any heart-shaped leaves with red tips."

"I'm guessing in here they prepare the plants for experiments," whispers Reggie.

Twisting my head to glance at where Reggie's voice came from, two people catch my eye. They have appeared from a room further down the corridor and are now walking quickly towards us.

"Hey Reggie, watch out behind you," I whisper, not knowing if he has seen them or not.

"We'll move the group back out to the light now," says the woman in the long white coat carrying a grey tray.

"Oh, no," whispers Reggie.

As they walk towards us, I step backwards, my hand still on Bella's arm. I'm trying to work out if they are going to walk straight into us or if they will miss us. Do I need to squash myself against the window or dive to the other side of the corridor!?

"Note the time before you take any samples," the woman finishes. Stopping suddenly in front of the door next to us, she pulls a card out from her pocket.

*BEEEEEEP*

*CLICK*

The door opens and they both quickly enter the room.

*CLICK*

I let out my breath. "I am NOT sure I can deal with any more people walking into us or *nearly* walking into us!"

Taking a few more deep breaths, my heart slows down from its rapid pounding. I look up and down the corridor and then through the glass at the two scientists. I know I have a superpower right now, but it's like I need eyes in the back of my head! Being invisible is hard work. With a few more glances to my left and right, I squeeze Bella's hand and then quietly watch through the window as the two scientists move around the room.

It is completely absorbing. One of them is collecting plants that have been under the white lights and the other is selecting equipment and putting it all on the table in the middle of the room. It's a bit like watching TV. They should make a TV show where you can't hear anything happening, you can only see people working in a lab.

"Hey," whispers Reggie, snapping me out of my daydream. "I think I can hear something. I think I can hear our school."

"Oh yeah," replies Bella after a moment's pause.

Somewhere further away from us and this quiet corridor, I can hear lots of joyful noises. There is definitely an excited chatting noise and maybe some laughing too. I can also hear a stern voice shouting WALK and STOP TALKING.

That *must* be our school.

And it is definitely further away from where we are standing.

"I think we are in the wrong section," I whisper.

"Yeah," laughs Reggie. "There is *no way* they would let us lot in here!"

Following the increasing noise, it doesn't take us long to find them. The voices we were actually following, as we quickly twisted through the corridors, turned out to be Year 3, loudly walking along in pairs. We wait for them to go past us, watching them all as we stand there silent and completely invisible.

In this part of the LABORATORY ZONE, there are no grey machines and people in blue plastic onesies.

Here, there are large rooms with large tables. It looks less high-tech and shiny, with more books and papers and chairs.

Passing empty room after empty room, I wonder if we have gone completely the wrong way. I'm just about to suggest turning around and following Year 3, when I spot Miss Tully and Year 4.

Through the window from the corridor, I can see that Year 4 has been sitting in groups around big round tables. There are sheets of papers all over the tables and as we walk past, they all stand up, pushing their chairs under the tables in front of them. Miss Tully is at the front of the room explaining something to them that I can't hear, and they are all watching her. That's the thing about these corridors – You can look through the windows at what is going on in the room, but you can't hear anything. It means that the corridors are quiet until a door is opened and then the corridor is flooded with noise.

"They're here!" whispers Bella, pulling my arm away from watching Year 4.

Yes, Year 5 is in the room next door!

I spot Mr Graveshead before I see the rest of them. His black hair is a big, shiny mess and his face is all screwed up and angry. He has his arms crossed in front of him, his shirt is creased and half untucked and his head keeps spinning around. I'm guessing he is doing his 'angry stare' at anyone who he thinks is talking. Mali is standing at the front of the room and looks to be explaining something as her arms and hands move around wildly in front of her.

"Look, there's Boatman," I whisper.

In the corner of the room, he is sitting on the edge of a table, looking down at his phone again.

"We need to get in," says Bella, "but we can't just open the door as it might be locked, or worse, Mr Graveshead will see it opening."

"Shall we try knocking?" asks Reggie.

"That only works with one person," I reply, "not a whole group like this. We don't want them all turning around and getting suspicious—"

"Hey, someone's coming out," interrupts Bella.

There is a woman in the room with a long white coat on. She has walked behind Mali and around a grumpy Mr Graveshead. Past Year 5, she's now heading towards the door in front of us. I can see she has a clipboard under her arm and a tray of empty glass beakers.

I take a big breath. "OK, let's try to do this delicately, without drawing attention."

My plan is simple enough: The woman will open the door towards herself, I'll then reach through and keep it pushed open. Then, the three of us will quickly sneak through after she's gone.

"Follow my lead," I whisper, ready to spring into action as I watch her get closer to the door.

Except, my plan doesn't quite work.

Quickly reaching out my hand, I leap towards the door as it opens to stop it from closing. As I leap, I manage to completely shove Bella straight into the door. I didn't realise she was standing there! Tumbling forward, Bella falls into the door as it opens. With the door now opening faster than expected, it swings straight into the woman coming through.

*BOOF!*

"Owwwww!" cries the woman as her hand slips and the door bashes into her forehead. She keeps hold of the tray of glass beakers in her left hand, but as her arm moves, she drops her clipboard.

*CRASH!*

"Everything OK?" Mali calls out as the whole room turns around to stare.

"Yes, silly door," replies the woman.

"OK, OK, you don't all need to watch!" shouts Mr Graveshead.

This is not the delicate, quiet and stealth-like operation I was hoping for.

*CLAP. CLAP. CLAP.*

"This way please," shouts Mali, still clapping her hands together.

While Mali gets the attention of Year 5 again, the woman in front of me reaches down to pick up her clipboard. Holding the tray steady and with her foot keeping the door held open, one beaker slips.

I jump forwards. Reaching my hand out for the falling beaker before it smashes on the floor, I fumble, but manage to grab it.

I wasn't really thinking.

"What?!" says the woman, as we both watch the floating beaker hovering just above the floor.

With nothing left to do, I gently place the beaker back on the tray again. At the same time, her jaw drops to the ground and her eyebrows raise high into her forehead.

# Chapter Fifteen

## With Great Power

Reggie, Bella and I are FINALLY with Year 5!
We are standing at the back of the room as they face Mali and listen to her. Mr Graveshead is on my left, still staring at anyone who speaks or moves, and Mr Netship is sitting against a table behind Mali, still looking down at his phone. I look at them both and then over to the large window on my right that leads out into the corridor. The woman with the tray of beakers is still standing there. She looks down at the magical beaker on her tray that has stopped

floating and then up at the door that mysteriously knocked into her.

That was close.

I take a deep breath as I watch her and then slowly breathe it out as she reluctantly walks away.

That was *too* close.

Turning back to face Mali, I quickly grip Bella's arm – we seem to be standing right behind Tammy and Charlotte.

"Books. Books. Books. Books. Urgh, people are always talking about books," moans Charlotte.

"Who are?" asks Tammy.

"Everyone! You know, teachers and, like, *her* at the front. Adults, like."

"Yeah… What's, like, the *worst* book, though?"

"All of them!"

"Mine is the dictionary. I mean, *boring*! It's just like words and meanings and things."

"Ha!" jumps in Anne, who is standing next to them. Her long brown hair falls down her back and as she turns, I can see she has an unidentifiable smudge on her cheek. If I had to guess, I would guess that it was chocolate. "I like the dictionary," she says, laughing to herself.

Tammy and Charlotte look at her with a mixture of confusion and boredom. Confusion: Like Anne is speaking a completely different language to them. Boredom: Like Anne is… Well, that's basically the usual look on their faces and has nothing to do with Anne talking.

Anne doesn't seem to notice or care, though. "You can look up words like 'bottom'," she says and then laughs again, her hands holding her stomach as she does so. "The lowest point or part of something," she says in a teacher-like voice, standing up straight with her index finger pointing up. "HAHAHA! It's fun!"

"She's right," whispers Reggie. "It is a good read."

Anne carries on chuckling and looks back at Mali, and Tammy and Charlotte continue with their confused-bored faces as if Anne hasn't just said anything to them at all. At the same time, I take a really quiet breath and step forward to stand closer to

Charlotte. This is the closest I have ever been to her. Usually, not that I ever really want to stand close to her, she would have spun around and given me a *look* that screws up her whole face as if there is a really bad smell in the room. I might be offended, except that I know I don't smell and that she does the same look to everyone, so maybe it is just her face.

Today, however, I am invisible.

I could poke them both in the back and they'd turn around and wonder what it was. That would totally freak them out.

"So, if you all follow me," shouts Mali at the front of the room. "Then I can take you to one of our many work rooms."

"A work room?!" groans Charlotte. "*That* sounds like *fun,*" she adds, her voice dripping with sarcasm that makes Tammy laugh.

Now I REALLY want to poke them both in the back. I want to scare them for being so completely rude and annoying about everything *all the time*. But, then again, as hard as it is to stop myself, I know I shouldn't. It's just like what Spider-man's Uncle Ben said, '*With great power comes great responsibility*'. He's right, of course – The power of invisibility needs to be used for good. This power needs to be used to save our school from whatever evil plan Mr Netship is up to.

Leading us into the next room, Mali starts again. "This room is mainly used for analysis and teaching."

"Boring," sighs Charlotte, throwing herself down onto the stool by the nearest table. Reggie, Bella and I stand behind her and as she puts her head down on the table in front of her in a huff, I hold my hands together tightly so there is no temptation to poke her in the back. Instead, I roll my eyes at her and then, because I know she can't see me, I do it again really slowly.

This new room is bigger. There are lots of tables in the middle and around the sides of the room. The tables in the middle have microscopes on them and the tables around the sides have books, piles of papers, large metal lamps, a computer and trays of equipment piled up.

"I have put some slides under the microscopes you see in front of you. Taking it in turns, I'd like you to have a look and say what you think you can see. They should all be in focus, but let me know if not."

With permission to move, everyone quickly migrates towards the microscopes. There is a lot of knocking and pushing as they all try to be the first or even the second in the queue.

"Ewwww, what is that!?" says Mila.

"You are looking at a leaf's stomata," says Mali with a chuckle in her voice as she stands next to her.

"Ewwww... Wait, what is that?"

"Very tiny pores on a leaf that allow carbon dioxide, water vapour and oxygen to get in and out."

"Oh, cool!"

Reggie, Bella and I need to get over to the other side of the room. Mr Netship is there and has once again found somewhere to lean. Unsurprisingly, he is staring at his phone again, with his long legs stretching out in front of him.

The trouble is, we need to get over there without

bumping into anyone.

With Reggie leading the way, we slowly work our way around the room, staying close to the tables along the sides and avoiding the tables in the middle. This is mainly OK and a safe place to walk, except when there is a sudden jump up from a seat and a scuffle as the next person sits down. It's these sudden movements that make bumping into people a dangerous possibility.

"One at the time!" shouts Mr Graveshead.

A quick pull on my arm from Bella and I stumble to my right, avoiding May, who's darting towards a free microscope.

"Be careful with them!" Mr Graveshead yells.

"Mali, Mali, what is this?" shouts Grace from across the room.

"You don't need to touch them!" shouts Mr Graveshead, marching across the room toward Audrey and Charlie. "Just look through the lens!"

To avoid walking into Peter, I shuffle and quickly side-step. I then slide along the edge of the table as

Imelda heads straight towards me.

*THUMP! CLANK!*

"Oops," I hear Reggie whisper.

Sliding along the table ahead of me, I can see Reggie's knocked over a thick green hardback book, which bumped into a large metal lamp.

I look quickly around the room and check to see if anyone has noticed: Mr Graveshead has his arms crossed and is standing behind Charlie. Mali is talking to Grace. I look over to where Mr Netship is sitting, but he doesn't look like he has noticed anything going on in the room at all.

As my shoulders lower and my held breath escapes in one big burst, my eyes fall on Tammy – She's looking directly at the fallen book. My heart suddenly thumps hard in my chest.

"Quickly," I whisper to Bella, as I see Tammy slowly turning her whole body towards us, her forehead creasing and her eyes narrowing. "We need to keep moving."

"Ohhhh, dear," whispers Reggie

"I know," I reply as I watch Tammy slowly getting up from her stool. "I think Tammy is coming over."

"Errrrr, no, it's not that," says Reggie. "That's not what I'm talking about. It's this… look."

Reluctantly turning my head from watching Tammy, my eyes frantically scan the area, trying to work out what Reggie is talking about. Then I see it. Stopping the scream that wants to explode out of my mouth, I whisper, "What?!" instead.

"Oh no, Reggie," says Bella.

"I know," he replies.

It's Reggie's hand.

We can completely and utterly see Reggie's hand lying flat on the table.

# chapter Sixteen

## A Floating Hand

"WHAT is your hand doing?!" I say before I have to put my own hand over my mouth again.

Reggie's hand is there on the desk next to the fallen book and the metal lamp. It's not invisible at all. It's also completely armless.

"This is bad!" says Bella.

"It's the UV light! I must have put my hand under the lamp when I knocked the book over."

"That lamp is a UV light?" I question.

"Yes," replies Bella, as if this is the most perfectly

normal thing in the whole wide world.

"So, the light rays from the sun bring us back to normal and so does that lamp?"

"This lamp must have quite intense UV rays," whispers Reggie.

Looking at the purple light coming from the lamp next to Reggie, I see a white sticker with red writing on the base: WARNING – UV RAYS.

"Quickly, open that book and put it on top of your hand," says Bella. "We can't have a hand just floating around or sitting on a desk."

Like someone who suddenly remembers they are standing in a sinking canoe, I snap out of my fixed stare at Reggie's hand and my eyes dart back to Tammy. She's creeping towards us.

"Bella, we need to move," I say, nudging her. "Tammy… Look, she's heading this way."

"Oh no… OK, Reggie," she whispers, "you'd better stay here and keep your hand covered."

Edging around Reggie, who is adjusting the book to cover his hand, I keep my eyes on Tammy as a sick feeling rises up to my throat. Our plan is not going well.

"Tammy!" shouts Mr Graveshead from the other side of the room. "Where are you going? What are you doing?"

"I was just… I'm… ummm… moving to this microscope."

"Well, join that queue," he yells, waving his hand around but already looking at something else.

Bella and I are moving towards Mr Netship. He is still sitting against the table, his shoulders hunched over as he looks at his phone. His long body looks even longer as his legs stretch out in front of him, crossing at his ankles.

"Mr Graveshead," Tammy sings in a loud voice.

"Yes!"

"I'm wondering where Reggie, Bella and Clara are?" She looks over at the book that is hiding Reggie's hand before looking back at Charlotte. Immediately Charlotte jumps up, knocking Anne out of the way as she does so and strides over to where Tammy is standing.

"My turn!" shouts Anne, sitting down where Charlotte had been sitting in front of the microscope.

"Oh yes, I was wondering that too," says Charlotte with her fake sickly sweet voice, which basically means she's lying and hasn't noticed we're missing until now. "Where *are* they?"

Bella grips my arm and I look back at where we left Reggie behind. I can just about see his hand underneath the book. Mr Netship doesn't seem to have noticed anything going on and is certainly not listening to Tammy and Charlotte and the shouty Mr Graveshead. Leaning on the edge of the table, he carries on looking at his phone.

Mr Graveshead hasn't replied to Charlotte. He's frantically looking over all the heads in the room, his hand waving about in the air as his eyes move from one person to the next. It won't be long until he realises they're right. It won't be long until he starts shouting and getting angry.

It is absolutely now or never.

I hold my breath again and with Bella next to me, I get as close as I can to Mr Netship and get ready to grab his phone. This is our new plan: I grab the phone and if anything happens, Bella will trip him up. I didn't really have time to protest at this new plan as we edged away from Reggie.

'ALL IN PLACE' – The message on his phone says – 'WE WILL BE GONE IN 10 MINS.'

All in place. So, his plan is working.

Standing behind Mr Netship, I reach out to grab his phone, but he changes the screen. He has quickly opened up his emails and tapped on a folder called 'Merihal'. My hand hovers next to it as he quickly scrolls down and selects an email.

*'I can confirm that once the school has closed down, you will get your money straight away.'* I read. *'We will do the rest, and when we have finished, they will be begging us to buy the land off them.'*

I'm too shocked by what I've read to move. I read it again.

"Ha!" says Mr Netship to himself, absorbing the

agreement before closing the email. He then has another little chuckle to himself as he scrolls through the other emails in the folder.

I need to get his phone and I need to do it now. Bella grips my hand, the signal for me to grab his phone and make it do a little dance in front of him. The plan is that he'll be so surprised, he'll think he's imagining the whole thing and has probably been staring at his phone way too long. He'll rub his eyes like they do in films or he might even faint.

"Aghhhhhhhhhhh!"

There is a scream from the other side of the room.

"Aghhhhh! Aghhhhh! Aghhhhh! Aghhhhh!"

Other people are also screaming.

Just as I'm jumping at all the screaming, Mr Netship jumps too. Shooting up from leaning against the table, he drops his phone down next to him. A split second later, the phone magically starts to slide. It's moving across the table like it's on some super slippery oil. Reaching the end, it falls and hovers mid-air. Well done, Bella!

"Aghhhhh, she has A HAND!" someone shouts out, and I turn around instantly. "I think I'm going to be sick!"

The first thing I see as I spin round is Charlotte, laughing. She has Reggie's hand and has lifted it high above her head, gripping it by his wrist. Everyone else in the room is staring at it, pointing at it, or screaming at it.

# Chapter Seventeen

## Red Flashing Lights

There is a deafening alarm that cuts through the room and red lights flash in front of my eyes.

When the alarm started, I immediately thought it was just me and that only I could see and hear it. Seeing Reggie's hand floating high up in the air and Charlotte's hideous smug grin as she held it up, sent a sick feeling to my stomach as my heart jumped into my lungs.

Actually, it's not just me; Turns out the loud alarm

is going off in the whole building and the red lights are flashing in the corners of every room.

"The culprit is here!" Mali shouts into the radio in her hand. "Red Group. We're in Room 94."

I can also hear in amongst the loud alarm, Mr Graveshead shouting, too. "Charlotte, put that hand down!"

There's Mr Graveshead shouting at Charlotte, there are screams from some of Year 5 as they huddle by the door and there is someone trying to talk to Mali on the radio. There is A LOT of noise. And it doesn't help that the red lights keep flashing in my eyes.

"Aghhhhh," the screams start up again, getting louder.

"Owwwww!" yells Charlotte. "No, you don't!" she yells again and I turn to face her. Through the strobes of red light, I see Charlotte is now sitting on the floor, rubbing her right shin.

Reggie has escaped!

"Get him!" Charlotte shouts at Tammy.

Leaping forwards, Tammy leaves Charlotte on the

floor. The hand is moving. It darts one way and then another. Tammy leaps towards it but it moves again.

"Go, Reggie!" I whisper.

"Aghhhhh!"

The screams grow even louder as Reggie's hand moves quickly towards the door.

"Aghhhhh!"

Like a magical spell, those standing by the door split into two. Knocking to the sides and falling over the tables, a powerful force-field pushes them all out of the way as it moves towards the door.

For a moment, I can't see Reggie's hand. I can see the red lights still flashing in my eyes and I can see the screaming faces of those stumbling over stools. Moving to the other side of the room, they run away from the door, revealing Reggie's hand again down by the floor. The door isn't opening, though. The door handle is moving up and down, but the door is not opening.

Tammy and Charlotte edge closer to the door. On the other side, Mr Graveshead is also getting closer.

With a sudden pounce, he dives forwards, completely missing whatever it was that he was diving at and lands face-first into the closed door.

As the hand darts to the left, Tammy jumps. She moves like she wants to give the air in front of her a giant hug. Hugging the air tightly, it doesn't quite look like the air wants to be hugged. She wrestles with it, determined to continue the hug no matter how much it protests.

Charlotte creeps forward.

As Tammy wrestles, Charlotte watches for a moment. She then delivers one swift kick to the hugged air and grabs the floating hand.

No! They've got Reggie… again.

With Charlotte now gripping the floating hand and Tammy still hugging the air, a long body appears through the flashing red lights. Mr Netship glides in front of my eyes, across the room and heads towards them. Without him saying a word, Charlotte holds Reggie's floating hand still so he can take a closer look at it.

Then the alarm stops ringing.

An echo of the alarm lingers in my ears as I watch the chaos in the room. The flashing red lights in the corners of the room are still on. It's like someone has just pressed 'mute' on the TV: The alarm noise has gone, but the red lights are still flashing away as if the noise is still there.

*CLAP. CLAP. CLAP.*

Mali claps her hands loudly three times. As she raises her hands above her head, we all turn to face her and the room goes completely quiet. "Can everyone please listen?!" she shouts. "The safest place for us is outside in the sunshine. There is nothing to worry about. That floating hand is attached to a body," she says, looking at all the scared faces around the room. "We have a plant here at BioZone called vanishing red, that turns its attacker invisible. UV light will bring them back again."

"I wasn't attacking it!" interrupts Reggie, his voice sending a wave of gasps through the room. "I was just looking at it!"

"Reggie!" shouts Mr Graveshead. "You are in big trouble!"

Mr Netship clears his throat. "Annnnd," he says slowly, immediately sending the room silent again. Even Mali turns to look at him. He says 'and' in such a way that makes it sound like the most important word in the whole world that has ever been said. He also says 'and' in such a way that makes it sound like the worst word ever to be said, ever. "I imagine that young Reggie here was not alone. *Where*, I wonder, are Clara Jennings and Bella Lewis?"

I don't want to answer that question at all. Standing next to his floating phone, I want to stay completely and utterly quiet and pretend we are not here. I am sure there is a way we can sneak out of this room with his phone and run to Mrs Elliot, so she can help us.

"We are here!" shouts Bella.

Well, there goes that plan then!

"Then you two need to step outside too," says Mali gently.

# Chapter Eighteen

## To Stay Invisible

The sun shines through the glass door ahead of us, as Bella and I walk arm in arm towards it. The light hits the glass and sends an image of the door stretching out across the grey floor.

We are walking on our own with the rest of Year 5 ahead of us. No-one knows where we are and no-one can stare at us. Poor Reggie is at the front next to Mr Graveshead. He insisted that Reggie walk next to him with his hand out in front, so he knew where he was. Walking ahead of us, Reggie and Mr Graveshead step out into the bright sunshine.

Like a reflection appearing on the surface of the water, Reggie shimmers. Where once there was nothing, an outline of Reggie blurs and comes into focus. It is absolutely amazing – Reggie is back.

I look down at my invisible body and stare at the grey floor. I quite like being invisible. I like no-one looking at me or knowing that I'm here. No-one staring at me. No-one telling me I'm standing in the wrong place. I can look at what I want to look at. Not being told to stop looking out of the window. Not being told that I'm daydreaming when I should be listening. Not being told that I'm not listening when I am *actually* listening to everything they are saying, it's just that my face might not look like I am. I could stay like this. I could go through my whole life doing my own thing and standing where I want to stand.

I would, of course, use this power for good. Being invisible, I could become the ultimate spy. I could simply be quiet and no-one would know I'm there. It would be a simple life. A quiet life. A life where I could do no wrong. No-one looking at me. No-one expecting anything from me.

With these thoughts floating around my head, my feet slow down. Looking at the floor, I see the reflection of the door out in front of me and know that my feet must be so close to it.

As my feet stop, I feel Bella gently tug at my arm. "Hey, why have you... Oh Clara, you can't stay here. You can't stay here like this."

"Why not?" I whisper, even though I know the answer.

"We have to keep going."

Bella stops tugging my arm. I feel her holding it and gently waiting for me to move. Taking a big breath, knowing that she's right but also wishing she wasn't, I take a step forward.

I push the door open and look down at my arm. As soon as the hot sun reaches it, my skin tingles. The outline of my arm appears, the image becoming clearer the more I look at it, the blurriness coming into focus. It is completely mesmerising.

"There's Clara!" shouts Charlotte, and I look up to see everyone in Year 5 turn to look at me.

"And Bella!" shouts Tammy.

Bella is coming back too – there a blurry shimmering outline of her before I see her fully once again. I had got used to hearing her voice without seeing her. "Hi," I say with a smile.

"Hi," she laughs, smiling back at me.

"You two, come over here now!" shouts Mr Graveshead.

Walking slowly over to where Mr Graveshead is standing, I can see the car park filling up with the different year groups of Green Grove School. I can see them coming out of different doors and being directed to different parts of the car park. There are crowds of people in long white coats and others in dark suits and coloured shirts.

We are the cause of all this chaos.

The whole of BioZone is outside in the sunshine because of us.

With the whole of Year 5 class staring at us and

some other groups turning around to stare too, I wish I was still invisible. Here and now there are about to be a whole heap of questions.

"What on earth do you three think you are playing at?" shouts Mr Graveshead. "We are on a school trip! Of all the people to cause problems on a school trip, you three are the *last* ones I would have expected to do this. What were you doing? Why were you away from the group? Why were you attacking a plant?"

"We weren't *attacking* the plant."

"How did you even get there?" he continues, ignoring Reggie. "Were the three of you made to do this? Was it a dare of some kind? How—"

"Mr Graveshead," I interrupt loudly, "they are really good questions. They're exactly the questions you should ask but they're not the *right* questions."

"What?!" he asks, staring at me while blinking rapidly.

"The right questions to ask, are questions we should have *all* asked right at the beginning of the day."

"We should have?"

"To Boatman… I mean, Mr Netship," I reply.

At the sound of his name, Mr Netship looks at me with a cold hard stare. It's a stare that could stop a rabbit mid-run, like the blinding light of a car's headlights. A stare that could be used to stop someone remembering their questions, and stop them remembering that with great power comes great responsibility. Not me. I could spend my whole life being invisible and I would be an awesome spy. I could change the world, watching people and stopping them from getting away with their evil plans. Or… Or I could stand in the bright sunshine of this spring day in a car park and ask them the questions that need to be asked. Here, right in front of them, where they can see me.

Bella was right all along: We need to stand in front of Mr Netship and ask him what is going on.

Teachers may not like it, but questions need to be asked. Scientists need to ask questions to discover things. Detectives need to ask questions to bring people to justice and solve crimes. Mr Netship needs to be brought to justice. Here and now, my Rule Number Two: No Questions, needs to be broken because questions must be asked.

"Mr Netship, why did you really bring the whole school on this trip today? Why did you ask Tammy and Charlotte to spy on us? Who is Merihal and why are they in our school right now? Why do you want them to make it look like our school building is unsafe? And why do you have an email on your phone that says they will pay you to permanently close the school?"

OK, that was a lot of questions.

I can't really believe all those questions came out of my mouth.

I didn't mean to ask so many and now everyone is staring at me and blinking really, really quickly.

Except Mr Netship.

His eyes and the corners of his mouth are twitching. His entire face is bubbling. He looks like a giant massive volcano that is about to erupt! The kind that scientists watch while holding their breaths. They evacuate everyone in its predicted path and then wait for their prediction to come true. There is about to be a full volcanic explosion and I am standing right in front of him.

"Why, Clara Jennings, would you ask me all these questions?" he says, and I can feel the ground shaking underneath my feet.

He steps towards me, and my heart fires off six quick beats, causing my lungs to panic. I immediately hold my breath as my throat tightens. I asked a question. I asked A LOT of questions. Let's face it, I asked way too many questions, and I asked them all to Mr Netship. What was I thinking?!

# Chapter Nineteen

## Vital Questions

"I trusted you," Mr Graveshead says in a quiet voice. It is a voice full of sadness and disappointment. He is not shouting. Mr Graveshead *always* shouts. I pull my eyes away from the volcano-bubbling Mr Netship and look up at him. I'm ready to meet a look that will mean we've done everything wrong and that we shouldn't have gone on our mission to find out the truth.

Except Mr Graveshead isn't looking at us. He is looking at Mr Netship.

He steps in-between us and the volcano-bubbling Mr Netship, turns and looks straight at him with his back to us. "I trusted you."

"What?" replies Mr Netship.

"I thought you had great ideas to help this school achieve better and bigger things. You said this school could be great again. You said you liked my ideas too. You liked my idea about a maths club."

Excuse me, a *maths club*? Come on! I've got loads of great ideas that would be awesome for our school, and not one of them involves creating a maths club.

"I trusted you and all this time you were just—"

"Mr Graveshead," growls Mr Netship. "Why would you believe them?"

"Were you lying to me?"

"He was, Mr Graveshead," cuts in Bella as we continue to stand behind him. "Mr Netship has a company called Merihal at school right now, while we're all out of the way. We were trying to find out what he was up to when we... umm... *mistakenly*... ummm... turned invisible... But it's all on his phone, emails and everything!" she says, bringing the phone out of her pocket. "He's getting paid to close down our school!"

"This is ludicrous," growls Mr Netship. "And that is *my* phone!"

Blocking him from retrieving his phone, Mr Graveshead continues to stand between him and us. "What is going on?"

"Can't you see these children are lying to you?"

"No, we're not!" Reggie cuts in. "You are."

"I want my phone back!"

Giving a small yelp, Bella jumps behind me and I jump behind Reggie.

"Bella," a gentle voice says to the left of us, causing the three of us to jump sideways. It's Mrs Elliot, smiling. "Can you please give *me* Mr Netship's phone so that I can give it back to him?"

"But, but, he's up to something at our school," protests Bella.

"His phone has all the evidence," I add.

"Yes, we all heard. Mrs Godden is on her phone

right now."

Looking around the car park at all the faces staring at us, I guess we have been quite loud, and I guess I kind of forgot that the entire school is still standing in the car park with us.

"Let's hand Mr Netship his phone and then we'll all get back on the coaches."

"He still hasn't answered my questions," I whisper quietly to Mrs Elliot as I try not to look at his burning red face behind an upset Mr Graveshead.

"And they were very good questions," she replies. "Excellent questions. In fact, I don't think I have heard so many questions from you. Perhaps you can start asking such vital questions in our science lessons... You know, just as long as they're relevant to what I'm teaching at the time and they don't take up the whole lesson." She finishes with a laugh.

In a sunny haze, I watch Mr Netship snatch his phone off Mrs Elliot and I watch her give the sternest look I have ever seen. Then I watch everyone in the car park turn away from us: Employees wander back into

BioZone, Year 1 class and Reception class form a queue, and then Year 2 join them. In the sunny haze of watching everyone, my head spins.

I asked A LOT of questions just then.

I asked questions and no-one rolled their eyes or tutted really loudly. Mr Netship was scary, yes, very scary, but Mr Graveshead didn't shout at me. He didn't make me stand there and answer my own questions or make me feel silly for asking them.

Yet, the biggest thought, the one that's sitting in the centre of my spinning head, is that Mrs Elliot – a teacher – thought my questions were *vital*. No good has ever come from asking a teacher a question… until now.

"Come on," says Bella, taking my arm again even though I can see her and her smiling face. "We'd better get on the coach."

\*\*\*

Sitting down at the front of the coach, I watch Mr Netship through the window, standing in the empty car park with Mrs Godden. As assistant head of the school, she thought it best to stay with him. I heard her tell the other teachers as I waited in the queue.

His face is completely red.

On the top of his bright red face, his blonde hair is sticking straight up and poking out the top. He's also back on his phone again, furiously hitting it with his finger before bringing it up to his ear. As soon as he sees me staring at him, I quickly turn away and immediately sink down in my seat so he can't see me. I turn just in time to see Mr Graveshead dragging himself onto the coach. Looking like someone who has just been told the worst lie ever, he doesn't look at any of us before he falls down on the seat, two rows in front of Bella and me.

"I can't stop staring at my hands," I whisper to Bella as the coach turns onto the fast road back to school. "You know, because they are here, and I can see them."

"That is exactly what I was thinking," replies Reggie with a nod. He's sitting on his own on the other side of the aisle from us. "That was weird for a moment, right?"

And he's right, it was. "But we did it," I say, feeling a big grin spreading across my face. "We did it. We stopped him," I whisper, so Mr Graveshead can't hear me. Luckily, it's very noisy on the coach because Mr Graveshead isn't shouting at everyone to be quiet. "We knew he was up to something and we stopped him."

"We did," Bella agrees.

"Do you think it will come back?" I whisper again to Reggie and Bella after the three of us have stopped staring at our hands.

"Mr Netship?" questions Reggie.

"No, the invisibility… Do you think it will come back?"

"Why would it come back?" questions Bella.

I can't help but notice that both of them are replying to my question with more questions! I try not to roll my eyes at them, because they do actually look genuinely confused. Instead, I take a few deep breaths.

I think their questions are allowed, seeing as the three of us are in a very confusing situation.

"Well," I begin, "let's face it, they said that there was still a lot to learn about this plant, right?"

"Yeaaaaaaah," says Reggie.

"So... maybe it never quite leaves you. Maybe the UV rays bring us back *for now,* but it never *really* quite goes away. Maybe... maybe it will happen again."

"I very much doubt it," replies Bella. "Unless Reggie decides to pick up another plant that turns its attacker invisible."

"Hey!" says Reggie, sitting up and leaning over the aisle towards Bella. "I was only trying to look at it!"

Bella turns towards him. "It was in a clear glass box. You can see through transparent glass!"

"Yeah, but not that much and it was kind of your fault really."

Tuning out of their argument, I look out the window again. Watching the blur of green trees as we pass them, with the different coloured fields in the distance, the sound of them arguing fades into the noise of everyone else on the coach.

I wonder if Bella is right.

*Maybe,* I think completely to myself. *Maybe she's right and it won't come back, ooorrrrr maybe, like the spider that bit Spider-man, maybe this plant has changed our DNA.*

# Chapter Twenty

## An Open Can

"**B**uilding repairs," Bella scoffs, as the three of us sit on our favourite red bench in the school playground.

It's Monday morning and I couldn't wait to get back to school. After the school closed for a week while the mice were cleared from the kitchen and the rest of the building was checked over properly, I was ready to come back. I had spent my week reading everything Mali had sent me about BioZone and the plant, vanishing red. There doesn't seem to be any research that shows if the invisibility comes back or not. What if it does? What if I'm like Spider-man now and my DNA has been changed? Reggie said I'm getting *'carried away'* and that of course it hasn't changed our DNA. Wish I hadn't told him now. Who really knows, though?

"I can't believe Merihal had hired Mr Netship to help make our school unsafe for us to be in!" continues Bella. "For Mr Netship to then close the school and send us all to different schools nearby."

"We knew he was up to something!" I shout.

It's nice to speak freely without pretending it's a yawn because of spies and lipreaders. I turn from watching Year 6 on the climbing frame to look at the window he used to stand at. No. It's OK. Mr Netship has definitely left our school for good.

"And then, I guess," I say, turning back to my friends, "the plan was that Merihal would sneak in, buy the land illegally and then knock the school down to build houses on. It's the same thing they keep doing."

"They have been building houses on the other side of town," adds Reggie. "Have you seen them? They look nice, but there's loads of things wrong with them. They also said they were going to put in two play-parks and a large allotment – you know, for people to grow vegetables and stuff. Apparently, they changed the plans at the last second and just put more houses there instead."

I shake my head and look out across the playground. "I can't believe they keep getting away with stuff like this."

"Well, they didn't get our school!" yells Bella.

"Yeah, but why aren't people questioning them, you know?" I say, turning towards her. "Why do companies like Merihal get away with this? Why do people let them?" I turn to look at Reggie and his wrinkled forehead. "There should be more companies like BioZone."

"Yes!" he shouts, clapping his hands together.

"Companies that question what is going on in the world and try to work out how to fix problems instead of creating new ones."

"Yes!" he says again with another clap.

"Companies that care."

Reggie pauses, looks down at his hands and back at me. "Do you think they'll *ever* let me go back there?"

"Ummmm," I say, trying not to look at his wide and hopeful eyes. "I think it might be best to leave it a little while longer before you ask."

"I was only *looking* at the plant," he mumbles, studying his hands again.

"Hey, it's great that Miss Hornsey is back," says Bella, successfully changing the subject.

"And Mr Graveshead seems to be back to normal," I add.

When the coaches arrived back at the school from BioZone, Mr Graveshead still wasn't shouting at anyone. Mrs Regan was the one who checked that we all got off the coach OK and Mrs Elliot was the one who went to talk to our parents. Mr Graveshead simply hung his head, looked at the floor, and quietly said 'goodbye' as he walked off to the school building.

It was so absolutely weird. I would say completely and utterly, hands-down, weirder than turning invisible. Today, however, he is back to shouting and I have never been happier to hear him shout for no reason other than he *always* shouts when he speaks.

"We have Mrs Elliot this afternoon," shrieks Reggie, snapping out of his grump. "She's going to go over everything we learnt at BioZone."

"Everything?" I question.

"Yep! I think mainly about the work they do with carbon dioxide… but she did say something about 'their other research and discoveries'."

"Then I am definitely going to ask a question," I say before bringing my right fist up to my mouth so I can bite it. "I think I will," I say through my fist. "Yes… Yes, I will."

As Bella laughs, I catch sight of two people in the far corner of the playground. It's Tammy and Charlotte. They have gone back to just watching us from a distance. I saw them watching us after assembly with Miss Hornsey. I saw them watching us when Mr

Graveshead stood shouting about our maths homework and I can see them watching us now. I think I'll continue to keep my eye on them.

"How were your doctor's appointments?" says Bella, looking at us both. "Mine was fine, and she said I was all OK."

"All good," Reggie and I chime together.

When we came off the coach, Mrs Elliot was ahead of us, ready to tell our parents. There was no way we were going to get away with it this time – Mum and Dad had to find out. I thought I was going to get told off. I definitely thought there was going to be something about me being grounded and not being able to do anything or watch TV. Nothing. Instead, they both went really quiet.

Darren also couldn't believe it. Elbowing me in the ribs, he whispered, "You are *so* lucky." I think he was just grumpy because he's in the middle of being grounded because of something he did two weeks ago.

I found Mum and Dad looking through all the information from BioZone for days afterwards. They also had the special doctor who needed to check me, explain it all to them over and over again. I honestly thought at one point the doctor would stop answering their questions. Instead, he repeated himself and they sat there nodding their heads very slowly.

Leaving the doctor, Mum and Dad didn't say anything as we walked down the busy corridor. It was only when we stepped outside in the sunshine that Mum turned to me. "Clara, I'm still not sure what has happened here," she said, shaking her head.

Pausing to allow a group to pass in front of us, Mum looked up at the clear blue sky. A bird flying over us caught our attention and we watched it land on a nearby tree.

"Yet," she began again as we continued to walk. "I have a horrible feeling that this may have opened up a whole new can of worms."

I simply smiled at her when she turned back to look at me.

*Sometimes,* I thought, as Mum, Dad and I continued to walk. *Sometimes, cans of worms need to be opened. Those worms need to be set free.*

Printed in Great Britain
by Amazon

85856973R00119